String of Fate

Jacob's Ladder

BIANCA D'ARC

This book is a work of fiction. The names, characters, places, and incidents are products of the writer's imagination or have been used fictitiously and are not to be construed as real. Any resemblance to persons, living or dead, actual events, locale or organizations is entirely coincidental.

No part of this book may be used or reproduced in any manner whatsoever without written permission, except in the case of brief quotations embodied in critical articles and reviews.

DEDICATION

This book is for all those who have stood by me for so very long. Especially my favorite Canadian, Peggy McChesney. Your support and willingness to be a cheerleader when I desperately need it are invaluable. And my friend, Anna-Marie Buchner, whose enthusiasm is contagious and much-needed. Thank you!

And special thanks to Suzanne and Shanda, who have gifted me with their friendship, enthusiasm and energy. You gals are fantastic! (And a lot of fun to hang out with!)

Special thanks to Dad for being my travel companion, goody-bag stuffer extraordinaire, and all around great guy. And to Mom for telling me years ago to "do what you love." Better advice, I've never heard.

.

DEDICATION

This book is for all those who have stood by me for so very long. Especially my favorite Canadian, Peggy McChesney. Your support and willingness to be a cheerleader when I desperately need it are invaluable. And my friend, Anna-Marie Buchner, whose enthusiasm is contagious and much-needed. Thank you!

And special thanks to Suzanne and Shanda, who have gifted me with their friendship, enthusiasm and energy. You gals are fantastic! (And a lot of fun to hang out with!)

Special thanks to Dad for being my travel companion, goody-bag stuffer extraordinaire, and all around great guy. And to Mom for telling me years ago to "do what you love." Better advice, I've never heard.

.

CHAPTER ONE

Ria was in serious trouble. Information was sometimes slow to get to her, but from what she understood, she wasn't the only monarch being targeted. No, someone was trying to take out all the shifter leadership around the world.

At the moment, she was pinned down inside the warehouse complex she and her Royal Guard protectors had been using as a base of operations for the past week. Ria really hated being always on the move with no permanent home, but until she found a way to hide the very potent magical charm that was a legacy of her position, her enemies would probably keep finding her. Sometimes, it felt like she had been running all her life.

In truth, it had only gotten really bad in the past few years. A few months ago, she had discovered one of the reasons why her enemies kept discovering her whereabouts. A traitor who had been ejected from the Clan for embezzling Clan funds had been selling information about her movements to the *Venifucus*—the ancient order that followed Elspeth, a fey witch who had been known as the Destroyer of Worlds the last time her evil was unleashed on the mortal realm.

Elspeth was in exile now. Had been for centuries. But her minions survived, looking for ways to bring her back from the forgotten realm to which she had been sentenced so long ago, when the forces of good had triumphed over her evil. Elspeth couldn't be killed. At least, nobody in the mortal realm during the last battle had known how to do it. She was at least part fey, with the fey's intense magic and near-immortal lifespan. Add to that Elspeth's extraordinary magic and she became close to unstoppable.

Thankfully, she *had* been stopped all those years ago, and Ria, among others, were doing everything in their power to see that Elspeth remained in exile. Her return to the mortal realm was nearly unthinkable. There was no doubt she would try to pick up where she had left off, subjugating humankind and shifters alike, killing thousands—maybe millions this time—in her quest for power.

And Ria, as Nyx of the *pantera noir*—queen of her people—held the secret to something that could soften the veil that separated the various realms of existence. As leader of the rare and deadly black panther shifters, she was also guardian of the intensely magical secret that had been passed down from generation to generation through her line. It was a secret the *Venifucus* somehow knew—or guessed. And it had made her a big, fat, favorite target.

"They're in the complex," Shelly, one of her loyal Royal Guards, reported in a tense voice. "We have to get you out of here now."

Ria was all for that. Whatever happened, she couldn't afford to be captured. If they got her, she wouldn't have much choice. She would have to take drastic action. She would die before willingly giving up the secret her family had held for a thousand years. It was that important. That vital to every living being in the mortal realm and beyond.

Though Ria was older than she appeared, she didn't want to die just yet. She hadn't even really begun to live. She wanted more time. Time to find a mate, fall in love and have little baby black panther shifters of her own to spoil...and to pass on the legacy of her line. That last bit sort of ruined the fairy tale, but she knew how important the guardianship was. Her ancestor had been chosen by the Goddess to be the guardian and Ria wasn't about to mess up a thousand years of obedience to the Mother of All's will.

Ria ran as fast as her human feet would let her, surrounded by her Royal Guard. There were only a few on duty at any given time, but those few were forces to be reckoned with and had saved her life many times before. The Royal Guard had prepared for every contingency before even considering actually using this location. As a result, they had an escape plan in place and more than one route to get out of the area.

Ria trusted her people to find her a safe passage, and if they came across any *Venifucus* soldiers, she and her Guard would take them out swiftly and silently.

Unless they were taken out first. So far, that had never happened. Somebody always survived to help guide her out, but that didn't mean she hadn't lost a few dear friends along the way. The lucky ones retired with injuries that made it impossible for them to continue as Guards. The unlucky ones went on to the next realm knowing they had done their duty, and she prayed for their souls on the other side of the veil.

Bronson was new to her Guard. He had come of age and finished his training just in time to replace her cousin, Cade. Though she missed Cade, she knew he had earned this time with his new mate, Ellie. Cade and his former fighting partner, Mitch, were both newly mated and now far from her side. She missed them dearly, but didn't begrudge them their happiness.

Ria had attended Mitch's recent wedding in Iceland and was truly happy for her former Guard. At that very same wedding reception, Ria had met a striking, startling, altogether scrumptious human male with a decidedly mystical bent. Ellie's older brother, Jake, had come to the party specifically to meet Ria—or so he had claimed. They had shared a dance and a bit of conversation that had haunted her for months now. He'd said he wanted to meet her because he was going to help her save the world.

Intriguing as that notion was, he hadn't wanted to

elaborate more than that. They had talked of many things that night, but had never returned to that rather outrageous claim. She had felt a bit like Cinderella at the ball. She had spent most of the night with Jake, as he'd told her to call him, but then, right around midnight, when the shifters began taking their furred forms and racing over the snowy, Icelandic volcano, he had disappeared.

She hadn't seen him since, but her thoughts had turned to him time and time again over the past few months. The simplest little thing would inspire memories of their few hours together and his delicious scent seemed to be forever embedded in her brain. She almost suspected...but no. He couldn't be her mate. He was human. And weird.

What kind of guy ran off like that? And what about that strange claim that he was going to help her save the world? Who spoke like that? She wasn't sure if he was as incredibly appealing as she remembered, or just some random fruitcake who led women on with cryptic words and then disappeared into the night, never to be seen again.

But if he was a fruitcake, why did she think of him almost every day? And why did she have this incredible urge to hunt him down? Why in the world did she want to see him again? He'd *left* her. Abandoned her like Cinderella had left the prince at the ball, holding nothing but a lousy shoe. Now that was some weird role reversal, wasn't it? And she didn't even have a smelly shoe to remember him by.

She was doing it again. Thinking about that encounter with Jake all those months ago when she had more important things going on. Right now, she should be concentrating on fleeing for her life.

She was following after Dorian, the point man of her small Guard detail as they headed for the closest of the pre-planned escape routes. Thank goodness her feet still managed to work even while her mind was on that damnable, disappearing man, Jake.

Ria was doing her best to move as quickly and silently as she had been trained, following in Dorian's wake. Shelly and her partner, Burgess, were on either side with Bronson bringing up the rear. And then Bronson cried out.

Ria spared a glance behind her to see the young man go down on one knee, then pop right back up again—bleeding. He'd been shot in the leg and from the sound of it, the gun was sporting a silencer. That was bad. Pros used silencers.

Bronson spun and began fighting hand to hand with the man who had come up behind him. Ria worried for the young Guard, but knew he was doing his duty and she had to do hers. She had to keep herself from being captured. It sucked being the black panther queen sometimes. Actually…all the time. Ria wasn't exactly a fairytale princess and doubted she ever would be.

For one thing, she was always on the run and had to watch her friends get hurt and even die protecting her and her legacy. Where was the fun in that? All it did was break her heart and make her live on pure adrenaline half the time, which was something she didn't really enjoy.

She ran faster, knowing Bronson was either already dead or gravely injured. His sacrifice would be for nothing if she didn't manage to escape.

Burgess fell back to take the rear guard position as the four of them kept running. They were in a long hallway filled with shadows. High windows on the left—an outside wall—allowed the weak moonlight to filter in from above, painting the scene with bizarre rectangles of light. Off to the right was the occasional connecting hall and a number of locked doors as they sped along. Her Guard knew which of the doors or hallways led to safety.

And then the shadows ahead moved. Dorian didn't cry out as he fell, but she knew he was down even as she heard Burgess engaging with more enemies behind her. Shelly moved in front of her and half-shifted to her battle form to engage with the enemy while Ria tried to look for another way out.

She didn't see any. No, they were well and truly trapped in the long hallway and this time, she truly thought her number was up.

With a crash, sparkling glass rained down on her from above and a rope hit the wall beside her. They were coming from above now too? She looked upward and saw a black-clad man silhouetted against the smashed window several yards above her head.

"Grab the rope if you want to live." The male voice drifted down to her—a voice she recognized from her dreams. It couldn't be... "Take the rope now," he urged, his voice low and steady.

Sizing up her choices, Ria realized there really was no other choice at the moment but to trust that her ears were not deceiving her. She reached for the rope.

A moment later, she was airborne, being hoisted at incredible speed toward the window.

Good thing she was a cat because when she got to the opening, she realized her knight in black armor was hanging upside down from the roofline. She jumped up onto the ledge of the window, twisted and then jumped upward once more, with her rescuer's strength helping her up onto the roof with him.

She caught a quick glimpse of his face and her breath caught. It was Jake. A Jake she had never seen before. Gone was the urbane man in a tailored suit, replaced by a tough-as-nails commando swathed in black.

"Come on. I've got a ride waiting." He dashed across the flat roof of the warehouse toward a ladder that led upward, Ria beside him.

For a moment, her panther wanted to jump for joy, running beside the man it had taken an instant liking to all those months ago. Her ears hadn't been deceiving her. This new Jake made her want to purr. He was tough and lean, muscled and dangerous. And he was here. Finally. Her very own male version of Cinderella.

She kept an eye out for enemies as they ran along, but the roof was surprisingly clear. Had the attackers left out this area in their coverage plan? If so, that was amateurish. They should have at least posted a sniper up here.

Then she saw a crumpled shape on the ground several yards ahead. As she neared, she saw that it was an enemy soldier. He looked unconscious and both his hands and feet had been bound with zip ties. Very professional work. Ria could only assume, as she kept on running, that Jake had downed the man on his way in.

She saw several more downed and trussed men along their path until they crept upward onto another section of the roof, this one a bit higher. For a human, Jake was remarkably fast. He seemed to be having no trouble at all keeping pace with her, which was exceptional. Ria was fast, even for a shifter.

Arriving on the upper level of the roof, she realized immediately why he had led her here. Twenty yards away was a small, black helicopter. Neither of them spoke as they raced for the chopper.

The night was dark, with hardly any moon, but Ria still saw the glint of light off a metal barrel to their right a split second before Jake knocked into her, altering her trajectory a tiny bit. He'd knocked her out of the path of a bullet, she realized belatedly, and he was returning fire even as he continued to run beside her.

She looked around, straining to see into the darkness. Even her cat's natural night vision couldn't detect anyone other than the single gunman, but she knew he would have friends on the way. They had to get out of there fast.

The gunshots weren't loud. No, both the attacker and Jake were using firearms equipped with silencers. She noted it with one part of her mind that wasn't set on escape. They were almost to the helicopter when one of Jake's shots hit its target. That attacker wouldn't be bothering them again.

Ria reached the chopper and climbed up into the small cockpit, while Jake did the same on the other side and quickly got the rotors moving. It didn't take long, but it felt like an eternity before they were in the air.

Gunfire followed them into the night, but Jake took the

bird almost straight up, leaving Ria's stomach momentarily far below. The sensation passed as adrenaline continued to pump through her system. She didn't have time to feel sick at the dizzying speed at which he shot out of range of the guys on the ground with guns.

He flew the helicopter up and outward, toward the open waters of the Atlantic Ocean.

Jake felt triumphant. He had gotten there in time to save Ria. For once in his life, his visions had given him time to do something about the shit that was about to hit the fan. His gift was a fickle thing. It often showed him what was to come, but either it was too close to the actual event or too vague for him to be able to identify when and where.

He had been seeing Ria in his visions of the future for more than a year now, though. He had been able to identify her at the wedding reception his sister had invited him to attend in Iceland. He still wasn't sure why his newly-mated sister had thought to invite him to the wedding of the tiger-shifter king at his stronghold. Humans—and clairvoyants—didn't usually mix with shifters. But his sister had married into the panther Clan when she'd mated with Cade.

Oddly enough, Cade was Ria's cousin. He had been a Royal Guard, protecting Ria, when he had crossed paths with Jake's little sister, Ellie. He saved her life. She helped him keep Ria—the queen of his people—safe and Ellie and Cade had fallen in love and married soon after. Jake had been in Asia during that whole episode, freaking out that his sister was in danger and he was too far away to help her.

That was one of the times his visions came too late to do any real good. He had tried to call and warn her, but communications had been very iffy where he'd been. When he had finally gotten through to leave a voicemail, it was after he'd already had another vision that showed everything working out okay. He had left that message but hadn't been sure she'd gotten it until much, much later.

Then Ellie's childhood friend, Gina, had been revealed as

a tiger shapeshifter. Jake had always known there was something a little different about Gina, but he had kept his mouth shut, knowing in his heart, Gina's secret was nothing bad. Gina had a pure heart, and her parents were downright spooky on the mystical level. Jake had only met them once, but that one occasion had been memorable.

Only now did he realize he had met the tiger king in exile. Gina was a tiger shifter princess and her new mate was the new king of all tiger shifters. His name was Mitch and he was also a former Royal Guard, like Cade. In fact, he had been Cade's partner, in service to protect Ria, the *pantera noir* queen. Her title was Nyx. Just like they called the tiger king the Tig'Ra. There was a complicated societal structure behind all the big cat shifter Clans that Jake was beginning to learn about through his sister and her husband—or mate, which was the term the shifters used.

Cade was only a cousin of the royal line, but if anything happened to Ria, he was in line to succeed as *pantera noir* monarch. Jake was certain that none of them wanted anything to happen to Ria. Being the queen of the black panther shifters was a heavy responsibility—even more so than Mitch's role as leader of the tiger shifters. There was something mysterious and weighty about the role the Nyx played in this that Jake didn't fully understand yet...but he would.

The visions were leading him somewhere and he figured by the end of this whole episode, he would know all of Ria's secrets.

He piloted the helicopter out to sea, surprised by Ria's silence. She had put on the headset that would allow them to communicate over the noise of the helicopter's engine, but she hadn't said a word since they left the rooftop. She had only stared out the window at the roiling seas far below.

Jake kicked himself mentally. She had probably lost friends in that warehouse. She was very close with those who guarded her day-to-day. They were not only her colleagues, but her friends. And it was possible at least one of them had died for her tonight. The others…well…Jake wasn't really sure of the health of the rest of her Royal Guard team. No doubt, several of them were badly injured, but there was one thing he could give her…

"Your Guard escaped," he said quietly over the headsets they both wore.

Ria's head swiveled so she could meet his gaze.

"What do you mean?"

"I mean that none of your Guard is being held prisoner by the people who tried to kill you tonight."

"How can you be so sure?" Her dark gaze was almost accusatory, but he was used to people being suspicious of his words.

He took a moment to tap his temple. "I saw it. Didn't Ellie tell you about me?"

"Tell me what about you?" Her gorgeous eyes narrowed.

Jake couldn't quite believe it. The one time he had counted on his little sister's blabbing mouth, she hadn't spilled the beans.

"I see the future, Ria," he said quietly, wondering how she was going to take his news.

She held his gaze for a beat before a smile broke over her face. She laughed and if the situation hadn't been so dire, he might have been enchanted by the tinkling sound of her amusement. As it was, he wasn't sure how to respond.

"Seriously? Is that the best you can come up with?" She laughed once more before subsiding. "You nearly sweep me off my feet at Mitch and Gina's wedding and then disappear, only to storm in—with a *helicopter*, no less—to save my life tonight, and that's how you're going to play it? You can see the future. Yeah, right. And I'm the queen of England."

"No, you're a queen of a much rarer kind. You're the Nyx, Ria. You control one of the gateways between realms."

The smile disappeared from her face. "Did Ellie tell you that? I should warn you, humans don't usually grasp all the nuances of shifter culture. She must've misunderstood something Cade told her."

Jake could see the anger in her eyes. Man, she was pretty when her eyes sparked like that, even if it meant someone was in trouble. She was probably wondering what her cousin had told his new mate, but Jake couldn't reassure Ria that her secret was still as safe as it had ever been until she believed him. He wasn't sure how he would convince her, but he had to keep trying.

"Ellie didn't tell me anything. I saw it. Starting over a year ago. Every month right around the new moon I saw the same thing, though it took me a few months to figure out the pattern. Every month I see you speaking for those in realms beyond. They come to the doorway and you listen and speak for them, but you always seem to miss the most important message of all. You've been ignoring the warning, Ria, and your spirit guardians have apparently decided it's time for some intervention. That would be me, I think."

"You can't be serious. You're speaking nonsense, like some New Age nutjob." She turned her face away, returning to staring out the window at the ocean below. Hmm. Well, Jake was nothing if not persistent. He had to get her to listen to him somehow.

"There's an older woman," he said after a moment's consideration. "She looks a heck of a lot like you. Why have you been ignoring her? She's been waiting at the portal, but you always take others before her."

Silence greeted his words and for a minute he thought he'd lost her, but then, slowly, she turned to look at him again, her eyes wide. "How do you know these things?"

"I told you. I'm clairvoyant. Always have been. I've gotten better at interpreting the things I see as I've grown older, but I've seen glimpses of the future pretty much all my life. Ask Ellie if you don't believe me. Even Gina knows about it. My gift was hard to hide from our closest friends growing up." If Ria wouldn't take the word of his sister—a human—she would probably give more credence to the testimony of a fellow shifter and monarch, his sister's best friend, Gina.

But Ria didn't say anything for a long moment. She merely

stared hard at him, her eyes narrowed.

She seemed on the verge of saying something that would tip the balance, but instead, she turned away. Her gaze sought the dark waters in front of the helicopter.

"Where are we going?" she asked, dodging the really tough topic of whether or not she believed his claim. He'd let her wriggle free...for now.

"There's a yacht awaiting our arrival," he said, adjusting a few controls as he began the approach that would take them to the helipad of the multi-million dollar craft.

"Really?" Her tone was suspicious. "You own a yacht?" That last bit had a definite, unspoken *yeah, right* after it.

"I never said it was mine. It belongs to a friend. A friend of yours too, actually. Samson Kinkaid loaned me the use of his yacht and helicopter when I asked."

"You know Sam?" Those lovely eyes of hers pinned him once more. How he wished he could erase the ever-present suspicion in them.

He would have to work on earning her trust. He wanted her to look at him as she did in his visions. But that would have to wait. He knew those particular glimpses of the future were nebulous at best. A lot would have to happen to make that part of the future into a reality.

"Sam and I go way back. We first met in Tibet. We studied together there for a while. We've been friends ever since, even though our paths don't cross often these days. I don't hang out with the jet set much." He smiled ruefully as he turned back to his controls. He could just see the yacht's lights in the distance, which meant Ria must have seen them already. He knew she had much sharper eyesight than he did. That was just one of the gifts of her shifter heritage.

"Tibet, huh? What were you studying there?" She kept her eyes focused ahead as she spoke.

"Life. Spirit. Martial arts," he answered with an inner grin. He would feed the curious cat, but on his terms. He'd spent enough time in Tibet to learn the art of being mystical.

"Where did you study? At a temple or something?"

"You could say that." He saw he was losing her interest, so he decided to drop another little tidbit. "It was the snowcat enclave, in fact."

Now he had her. She turned to look at him, her eyes wide. "No way."

He couldn't help the grin that spread over his face. "Way." He sensed she didn't quite believe him. "I'll take you there one day."

Damn. He hadn't meant to tell her that. He had seen them there, in that village high in the Himalayas. Together. It was one of his most precious visions because in that small snippet of a possible future, they were both happy and smiling, and the look in her eyes as she gazed at him held a kind of love he had never experienced.

He wanted that. He wanted to make that future into a reality. Had he ruined his chances by saying too much?

"Of course you will. And then I'll fly to the moon on the back of my pet pegasus." She seemed to let the comment pass, turning back to the lights that were growing ever clearer as they approached the yacht.

Jake let the silence stretch as he brought the helicopter in for a landing on the helipad positioned on one end of the giant yacht. He didn't radio the captain, having already alerted the man that he would be running silent, but the man had his crew ready and waiting to secure the chopper when they landed.

Ria didn't need any instruction on when and how to get out of the helicopter and she seemed to assess everyone she saw before her gaze came back to rest on Jake. She joined him near the stairs that led down from the helipad to the deck.

"What now?" she asked. There was no trace of what she might be thinking or feeling in her voice. No, she was all business. Calm, cool and collected. Even after what they'd just been through. Jake wanted to break through that composure, but knew it would take time.

"First, we check with the captain to see if there's any word from the shore. I left a watcher in place to let us know what happened after our departure. If all went as planned, there should be a report waiting for us. Then perhaps we can scrounge up something to eat. Or would you rather rest in your state room?"

"Let's go to the captain then. I want to know what happened back there."

"Your wish is my command." He bowed slightly, unable to help the little bit of humor that kept wanting to come out. He was finally here. With her. Doing the things he had only seen in his visions to this point. It felt good to have the pivotal moments behind him—at least for now.

She was safe and with him. He would do his best to keep her that way.

CHAPTER TWO

Ria had known in a roundabout way that Sam Kinkaid was loaded, but the opulence of his yacht still sort of blew her away. They walked down the stairs from the helipad, escorted by a silent, polite warrior. There was no doubt the man was a shifter and some kind of highly trained soldier. Whether he was there to protect her or just solely to protect Sam's property, she didn't know, but either way, he was an imposing presence.

The man had nodded once to Jake as they neared and then turned to escort them to the bridge. There had been respect in the gesture that wasn't something Ria would have expected, given the fact that Jake was undeniably human. His scent was that of pine and incense. A mystical blend that was slightly intoxicating, but still absolutely human. Maybe a little magical, but not in the usual sense of the word.

Maybe he really was clairvoyant, but Ria wasn't putting any money on that claim. Not yet. He would have to prove himself to her before she believed that sort of thing. True seers were rarer than rare.

Their escort smelled of big cat. Not panther, but possibly lion. Maybe tiger. He was staying downwind and at a slight distance so it was hard for her to get a good read on his scent, but he was definitely a shifter.

She didn't feel any imminent threat from him. Quite the opposite in fact. She knew Sam Kinkaid well enough to give the benefit of the doubt to any shifter he hired to be part of his personal crew, but she would keep her eyes open. Trust, but verify was something she'd learned from a human leader that had always made a lot of sense to her. Shifters were, at times, subject to the vagaries of their animal natures. It made sense to keep one eye on any new predator in the area.

And this strange warrior was most definitely a predator of the first order.

He seemed to respect Jake, though. It almost felt as if he already knew the human. Like they had some shared history. She would have to get to the bottom of the mystery there. It wasn't often that humans mixed with shifters as easily as Jake appeared to. He seemed perfectly at home with her dual nature and didn't even blink at the cat-shifter warrior who had met them at the helipad.

She would have to investigate the reasons behind that a little further. Her curiosity was piqued and like all cats, her curiosity was something that demanded satisfaction. She would get to the bottom of the mysterious human who has rescued her sooner or later.

They arrived at the bridge and their escort stayed just at the doorway while Jake ushered her inside as if he, not Sam Kinkaid, owned the place. He shook hands with the captain like an old friend, then turned to introduce her, but she needed no introduction to the big man who stood near the helm. She moved into his open arms with an audible sigh of relief. If there was anyone on earth she could trust to help her in this dire situation, it was the captain of this ship.

"Uncle Ed," she smiled as she hugged the older man. "I always knew you were a pirate, but when did you take to the high seas?" She stepped back, out of his embrace, but didn't go far. She was aware of Jake at her back, but the reunion with one of her favorite teachers took precedence.

"Little Ria, you've blossomed into a fine young queen. It's been too long." He held her at arm's length, looking her over as if to make sure she was whole and undamaged. "But I hear you take too many risks, sweetheart. What good is all your training if you aren't around to use it?"

"I guess you two already know each other." Ria heard the slight bristling in Jake's tone.

If he had been a shifter, she might've thought he was staking a claim—albeit a light one—but Jake was human. They didn't do such things, did they? She didn't know enough about humans to really know for certain.

"Little Ria was one of my best students, back in the day," Edvard replied, transferring Ria to stand next to him, his big arm looped over her shoulders, tucking her into his side.

She felt safe and protected by the older man. She always had. Edvard Grantham wasn't her uncle by blood, but he had taken her under his rather enormous wing and taught her everything she knew about firearms and navigation over land and sea.

Edvard was Sam's uncle. They were related by the fact that Sam's father had a sister who had fallen in love outside her own species—with Edvard Grantham. Their children were very powerful shifters. Some were selkies, like Edvard—seal shifters that were highly magical and very long-lived. Edvard himself was much older than he looked. With the sheer volume of magic coursing through his veins, he would likely live for many more centuries.

"I didn't realize you were a teacher," Jake said, challenge clear in his tone, but Ed only grinned wider.

"There's a lot you don't know about me, Seer. And a lot you'll probably discover in time. So my sister says and I've never had reason to doubt her vision." Edvard's words startled Ria.

It was rumored Ed's sister, Sophia, was a true foreseer, but she lived in seclusion. Ria didn't know for certain if the tales were true, but the very fact that Ed had called Jake a seer raised both her eyebrows and her suspicions.

If anyone would know if Jake's claims at clairvoyance were true, it would be Edvard Grantham. He alone was the only person Ria knew who actually might know someone with that rarest of magical gifts. If the rumors were true.

Things were starting to get interesting. If Jake was telling the truth…well…a lot of her assumptions would have to change. And his words all those months ago at the tiger king's wedding were racing around in her mind. He'd said that he was going to help her save the world.

Sweet Mother of All. If he really did see the future, they were probably in for a rocky ride.

Jake didn't like the way the yacht's captain held Ria so familiarly. He felt a little frisson of both envy and jealousy rear up inside him that he was powerless to stop. He did his best to control it, but he knew damn well that Edvard saw right through his words and body language. Damn. Jake didn't like being so transparent. He had worked long and hard to be as inscrutable and unreadable as any shifter.

But apparently all it took was one little woman to shake his hard-won cool. Ria made him forget all the training and the work he'd put in to gain respect among these powerful warriors. Most of them were born with native animal abilities that he'd had to work his ass off to duplicate, though never surpass.

Jake could fight alongside the best of the shifters now, but he would never have the same speed and reflexes they came by naturally. He was merely human, while they had inner animal spirits to call on and strengthen them. Jake had to rely solely on his training and the stubborn, subtle magic he had worked years to make behave.

He wasn't a mage in the usual sense. He didn't do spells or incantations. The magic wasn't something he used like a tool. Rather, his special brand of magic *used him*. It worked its will in his mind and body, allowing him to see things that had not yet happened. It was a wild magic that he had tried for years to tame. Only occasionally did it break the bonds he had put on it and have its way with him.

And when that happened, it was usually for a very good

reason. Those episodes led to some of his greatest, most urgent prophecies.

But the rest of the time, he was just a highly-trained, warrior human. No different from the usual Spec Ops guys some of the shifter soldiers had worked with and befriended when they had been in the armed services. Only, because of Jake's unique gift, he had known about shifters from an early age. There was no hiding the dual nature of the animal spirit from Jake's unique vision.

He had been fortunate enough to find trusted teachers who could set him on the path he knew he had to take. All his life, he had worked toward these events that were beginning to unfold now. He couldn't see every minute detail, but he knew things were progressing to the nexus point he had been born to foretell and forestall...if at all possible.

He had been born to protect the Nyx.

Only she was going to be a hard woman to convince. But that was okay. Jake liked a challenge.

"And you, my young friend," the captain turned to him, Ria still tucked familiarly under his massive arm. "I am glad to see you live up to your reputation. Sam told me to give you whatever you wanted and let you do your thing. We shall dine together tonight and I will grill you mercilessly for all your secrets." He gave a booming laugh and finally released Ria, who was actually giggling.

"He means it too," she added. "Uncle Ed has probably forgotten more about interrogation than we'll ever know." That she dared to tweak the older man's pride with such casual teasing meant there was a history between them.

Jake calmed a bit at the way she referred to him—twice now—as her uncle. Perhaps his familiarity was merely a paternal sort of affection based on a shared past. Somehow that was easier to take than the idea that she was attracted to the huge shifter.

Jake merely nodded, unsure how to respond. He had met the captain only briefly before setting off on his mission to rescue Ria. He'd known the man was extremely skeptical and really didn't understand why Sam put so much faith in a mere human, but he hadn't had the time or inclination to explain. Jake had learned over the years that actions often spoke louder than words.

Nobody had known why exactly Jake had needed to borrow Sam's helicopter and yacht. Not even Sam. It was a testament to their friendship that Sam hadn't asked questions when Jake called in the middle of the night and asked for the huge favor. Not even the captain had known where Jake was going or who he would be bringing back, but it had worked out even better than Jake had hoped. Not only did the older man have sympathy for another shifter in trouble, but he knew Ria and held her in high regard if his reaction was anything to go by.

A ringing tone sounded through the bridge. There was a woman at one of the consoles who quickly accepted the transmission. Jake hadn't seen her before, but he knew she was probably another shifter—one of Sam's kin or staff, or both.

"Captain, it's a call from shore asking for someone named Jake." Her delicate eyebrow rose as she looked in Jake's direction. They hadn't been introduced so she was just putting two and two together. Smart girl.

"That'll probably be my man on shore, reporting in about Ria's people," Jake said in a low voice, knowing the shifters all had superior hearing. No need to shout around these people.

"Put it on the speaker please," Ria ordered, leaving Edvard's side to move closer to the woman and her console of complicated controls.

Jake moved next to her, touching her arm. "Are you sure you want to hear this?" Jake knew in all likelihood, she had lost friends in the action tonight. His watcher likely wouldn't know she was listening and wouldn't soften the words of his report.

Ria's eyes closed for a single moment as she seemed to steel herself. "I must."

He had to admire her strength, even if he disagreed with the idea that she had to face everything alone. She would soon learn that he would be at her side, ready to share her burdens…for as long as she would let him.

"All right then." He nodded to the woman and she flipped a switch.

"You're on speaker," the woman said softly.

"Jake?" A man's voice came over the speakers in the wheelhouse.

"I'm here. We're safe. What happened after we left?" Jake almost dreaded the casualty report, but he needed to know what the enemy had done after their prize had been stolen out from under their noses. The enemy's reaction would dictate his next move.

"As you might expect, once they realized she was gone, they left rapidly. Only a small crew remained to sift through the scene for clues as to where she might've gone. I don't think they found anything. They hung around for a while, but left after reporting in their lack of progress. I believe you got away clean."

"What about casualties?" Ria blurted. Jake understood the slight edge of desperation in her tone. From what he understood, her Royal Guards were also her dear friends, with her every day, at all times. Losing one would be like losing a member of her extended family.

"Three injured. One seriously. I took the liberty of helping them out of the warehouse and giving them a hand finding an understanding shifter medic."

"Who are you?" Ria breathed, confusion and relief warring in her voice.

"Sorry, ma'am. My name is Ben. Jake can tell you more. I've been aware of your existence for a while and am happy to be able to help. Your people are safe. I can give you a call back in about an hour from their location if you want to speak with them."

"I would love that. Thank you, Ben. And thank you for helping my friends."

"It's my pleasure, ma'am. Glad I could be part of this op, in even a small way. I'll call back in 57 minutes. Jake, if you need anything else, you know where to find me."

"Roger that. Thanks, Ben. Call before if there are any changes."

"Will do." He hung up without much further ado and the line went to static before the female shifter at the console turned off the speakers.

Ria sagged with relief. "I thought for sure I'd lost Bronson. He was so green. Fresh from training and only in my employ for a few months."

"Ben said he was injured. He's not dead and he's getting medical help. He'll be okay," Jake tried to console her. He really wanted to put his arm around her shoulders the way the captain had earlier, but he was afraid she would pull away. It was too soon to take liberties...even small ones like that.

Jake knew he had to be patient. She shared her soul with a cat and the panther inside her was going to be harder to convince than the human—or so he feared. He had to approach her slowly and let her get to know him. Let the cat come to accept him.

And then she turned toward him and walked straight into his arms.

Or maybe he was all wrong about the cat thing. Maybe she just needed to be held after the ordeal she had been through tonight. Jake hugged her close, resting his head above hers, allowing her to draw comfort from his embrace as he nearly forgot to breathe at having her so close.

She felt so right in his arms.

"Dinner is ready," the calm female voice intruded on their moment and Ria pulled away. Jake wanted to curse the efficient woman who was still manning her console, but he had to let Ria go.

"Come on," Ed's voice reached them across the length of the bridge. He had moved toward the doorway and was waiting for them. "Some sustenance will set you right again, my girl. And after that, your friends will likely want a word with you and you'll find all is well before seeking your bed for the night. Things will be brighter in the morning." He smiled at his own words as he ushered them out of the wheelhouse and down toward one of the dining areas on the gigantic yacht.

To say the yacht was luxurious would be an understatement. They were led to a dining area that was just one of many on the big ship. This one was open to the night air on the stern, and more casual than Ria had expected. The gentle motion of the ship was soothing as she sat and the first course was served.

The plates were fine china and the goblets crystal. The silverware wasn't silver, but what looked like it could be either a very thick gold plate or perhaps even solid gold. If anyone could afford such things, it would be Sam Kinkaid, Texas oil baron and—through a strange quirk of fate and heritage—king of all lion shifters.

They ate quietly at first. Ria realized only as the steaming hot beef soup was placed in front of her that it had been quite some time since her last meal. Her inner panther appreciated the successive courses, which all had some kind of meat or fish involved in their creation. It was a feast fit for a carnivore, which probably was most of the crew, now that she thought about it.

Edvard was a selkie—he could turn into a seal and had very magical powers compared to other kinds of shifters. There were probably a few other selkies among the crew, and a bunch of lions as well. The jury was still out on the soldier who had met them at the helipad, though she was leaning toward thinking he was a tiger. If she saw him again on this giant yacht, she would try to find out if her guess was correct.

Ria began to slow down as the food began to really hit her digestive system. Her body was glad of the sustenance and now that it was sure more was on the way, she was able to slow down a bit. She looked up from her plate and realized the men had been talking quietly around her while she was focused so completely on the delicious food. She wiped her mouth with the snowy white linen napkin and met Edvard's gaze with a small, slightly self-conscious smile.

"My apologies, gentlemen. It has been a while since I last ate. Please forgive my poor manners."

"Nonsense, lass," Edvard answered heartily, sending her an understanding smile. "Feed your beast and then the human side can try to reason out our next move."

"*Our* next move?" She emphasized that first word as she repeated the phrase. "I hadn't realized you intended to do more than you already have. Believe me, I'm entirely grateful that you were able to offer us a safe haven for the moment, but I don't want to bring even more danger to your doorstep...or gangplank, as the case may be." She looked around at the yacht with a bit of humor. Edvard smiled back at her.

"Danger is my middle name," the older man scoffed. "Didn't I tell you that way back when we first met?"

He had, in fact, said exactly that to her all those years ago. It was a running joke with them and it felt good to be reminded of those early days when her burdens weren't quite so great.

"Nevertheless, you need to realize that giving me safe harbor could put you and your crew in real danger. I have been pursued most of my life, but the action lately is worse than it's ever been." She didn't understand what had caused the recent escalation, but there was no denying things had gotten exponentially worse for her since her aborted attempt to move to New York City a while back.

Her cousin, Cade, had found his mate during that debacle, so that was one good thing to come out of it. But others had been lost. Precious souls. Friends. And Cade had his mate to think of now. He no longer served as one of Ria's Royal Guard. He was too busy taking care of his mate and setting up a home for them both.

Cade's partner, Mitch, had also been lost to her service at the same time. He had been gravely injured. Poisoned, in fact.

He had almost died—and would have—if not for the attentions of the woman he had discovered and claimed shortly thereafter. His new mate, Gina, was not only a doctor, but born and bred tiger shifter royalty.

Mitch had been touched by the Goddess during his healing and had somehow ended up becoming the Tig'Ra—the tiger shifter king. He lived in Iceland now, at the traditional seat of tiger shifter power, on the side of an active volcano. He also had a penthouse in New York and he and his new mate were working hard to clean up the mess left behind by the usurper who had ruled over the tiger Clan by deceit for decades.

"I might be able to shed some light on why the violence has escalated recently," Jake said quietly from the other side of the table.

Ria had avoided looking at him, but she couldn't do so any longer. Something about Jake's cool, steady gaze sent little tingles through her body. It wasn't exactly uncomfortable, but it was something she didn't understand and wasn't really prepared to deal with. She had lived her life mostly on the run. She had never really had time to date or be in a relationship. Nothing that lasted, at any rate.

In all the ways that counted, she was as green as a young girl when it came to men. And human men in particular, were a mostly unknown quantity. Ria was surrounded by shifters all the time. Her Guard were shifters. Her friends were shifters. There was a protective wall of shifters between her and the rest of the world—and humans in particular.

Ria saw Edvard angle his body to look hard at Jake too, but the human didn't even fidget under the scrutiny of the powerful selkie's regard. No, Jake seemed to be made of stronger stuff than that. He wasn't cowed by Edvard and he had already proven how capable he was of spiriting her away from danger. If not for Jake, she would probably be dead right now.

"I've been in touch with the Lords of the Were in North America, South America, Europe and Asia. I'm also in close contact with a friend in the snowcat enclave in Tibet. Those of us with foresight, and those who have access to foreseers, all seem to be seeing the same thing. Danger. Threat. The specter of massive violence against all leaders of shifters everywhere. As you probably know, there were a series of consecutive attacks on shifter monarchs all over the world, timed perfectly as a distraction."

"Distraction from what?" Ria wanted to know.

"An attempt to divert the power of a volcano in the Pacific Northwest to influence the veil between worlds." Silence met his words. "This has actually been attempted twice now. First at the site of the tiger stronghold in Iceland, and the most recent attempt in the Cascade Mountains. Mount Baker, near the Canadian border, has come to life for the first time in decades. That was the second attempt to divert the enormous power of a volcano that was, thankfully, interrupted at the last moment. We speculate that the *Venifucus* are getting bolder in their attempts to bring down the barrier between worlds, and return Elspeth from the farthest realms to the mortal plane. Which is why they're after you in a big way, Ria, I'm sorry to say. The power you control is very tempting to those who would use it for evil purposes."

Edvard's gaze shifted to Ria, making her want to squirm in her seat, but she held her ground. Edvard knew about her abilities—as most shifters did—but not where they came from.

"It is said that the Nyx speaks for the departed," Edvard said quietly into the ocean night. "But does it go beyond speaking? Can it? Can they use you to break through the veil, Ria?"

She didn't know what to say. She didn't want to lie to her old mentor, but she couldn't say too much. The secret was important to keep. The silence dragged and that seemed to be answer enough for the big selkie. His lips thinned as he ground his teeth together and a hard look came over his face as he realized what her silence meant.

"It is the blessing and curse of being the Nyx," Jake went

26

on, speaking for her as if it were second nature. As if he knew all her secrets.

Edvard looked sharply at Jake. "Then it is even more important to protect her, whatever the cost."

She didn't like the sound of that. "Too many have already died for me and the secrets I keep," Ria said softly, drawing the attention of both men. "If I am ever put in a no-win situation, I will take my secrets to my grave and, with any luck, that will be the end of it."

"While your dedication is admirable," Jake said with no humor at all, "if we are very cautious, it won't come to that."

"You've foreseen it?" Edvard asked quickly, as if he truly believed in Jake's claims of clairvoyance.

"I see many possibilities. Not all end in Ria's death. And some end in even worse disaster."

"What could be worse?" Edvard asked, realization dawning in his eyes even as he finished speaking. "You mean...Elspeth? Here? On earth?"

"It is one of many possibilities and at this point, I'm relieved to say that most of the divergent lines of fate don't end that way. The odds are good that we can still avert it. Surely your sister has told you the same?" Jake turned the tables on Edvard, asking a question of his own.

The ship's captain cringed and looked away in an unaccustomed show of vulnerability. "She is not speaking to me at the moment."

Jake grinned a little, his expression understanding. "I understand. I have a sister too. We don't always see eye to eye." Edvard looked back at Jake and nodded, sharing the slight smile. "You should reach out to her. Chances are she's just waiting for you to make the first move."

Edvard nodded once, as if making up his mind. "I will call her tonight. This is too important to let a little family disagreement interfere with the flow of intel."

Ria shook her head. She sometimes forgot about Edvard's military background. He was such a teddy bear most of the time—and especially fatherly with her—that she forgot about his warrior skills and the hard life he had lived prior to the ascension of his nephew to the lion throne. It hadn't been an easy life for any of the Kinkaid line before then, and tensions still occasionally revved a little too high among the lion Prides even now.

"For now, we're safe at sea, but we'll have to put in to port eventually," Edvard continued after a moment's pause. "Have you given any thought to where you want to go?"

That one she could answer. "I don't want to bring trouble to any of my friends or allies, but I think now is the time when I need them most. Is it possible to establish secure communications with my cousin, Cade, and maybe Mitch, the new tiger king, too? I'd like to talk to them first before I go any further."

"That's easy enough. We have a full communications suite here and a dedicated war room down below. You should know I also have a platoon of my kind patrolling the waters around our position at all times. You might see some of them coming aboard or going over the side occasionally."

"Good to know." She nodded, trying to hide her surprise that so many selkies were concentrated here. Was that normal or something Edvard, Sam, or even Jake, had arranged just for her?

"And we have shifters of other kinds manning the ship. Every person you see acting as an employee on this ship—from chambermaid to mechanic—is a highly trained warrior. Most are lions, but we have a few tigers and other assorted species that enjoy the water. If you run into trouble, they can help."

Ria nodded again. She was glad that the folks around her were able to protect themselves with the way trouble seemed to dog her steps everywhere lately. She hadn't had a break in way too long. Even this quiet dinner was something to be savored. In recent weeks, she had been eating on the run more often than not.

"Captain, the man named Ben has called back, asking for Jake." The woman from the bridge had come down to the dining area with a small tabletop communications device in her hands. She plugged it in to the receptacle discretely hidden under a small panel and connected the line. "Go ahead," she instructed once the line was open. "This connection is as secure as we can make it."

"Jake?" Ben's disembodied voice came through loud and clear over the conferencing system that allowed everyone to hear as well as be heard on the other end.

"We're here, Ben. How'd you make out?" Jake asked.

"I'm at the healer's with the Guards. Everybody's okay. The one kid will need a bit of time to get back on his feet, but he'll be all right. If their employer is around, they'd like to speak with her."

"And I want to talk to them too," Ria said, directing her voice toward the speaker that sat in the middle of the table.

"I'll hand the phone to Dorian," Ben replied.

A moment later Dorian's voice came over the speaker. Ria hadn't realized until that moment that she'd been holding her breath.

"Who's there?" Dorian asked, his habitual suspicion making Ria smile, though he couldn't see her.

"It's me Dor. How are you guys?" Ria replied in a voice that was, surprisingly, a little choked up.

"We're fine. Are you safe?" Dorian always put her safety first. It was just one of the reasons he was one of her elite Royal Guards.

"Safer than you at the moment. I'm in good hands, Dor. Don't worry about me. Now, please, give me details. What happened after I was swept away from the action?"

"Milady, you scared the shi—heck—out of us, if you'll pardon my saying so. One minute you were in the center of our formation, the next you were gone and all I saw was your foot disappearing through the window up top. How the heck did you get up there?"

"I had a little help," she answered, though she was more interested in what had happened to her team after she'd left. "A friend came to my—our—rescue. I don't think any of us would have made it out otherwise."

"I hate to say it, but you're right. The moment the attackers realized you were gone, they broke off. We did our best to delay them so you could get away, though next time, I really wish you'd tell us if you plan to take a scenic tour of the roof."

Ria laughed. "I promise, Dor. If there's time. Though this wasn't planned. At least not on my part. We're just lucky the cavalry arrived."

"Luck had little to do with it," Edvard broke into the conversation. "The man who rescued you is a seer. He knew where he had to be and he made it happen." Edvard shifted around in his seat, as if uncomfortable with something, but he didn't let it stop him from continuing to speak. "Dorian, this is Edvard," he addressed the open phone line. "Are you still dropping your left when you move in to strike?"

"Ed?" Dorian's voice held a hint of both disbelief and pleased surprise. "Oh, thank the Goddess she's with you. You'll keep her safe."

"Yes, I will," Edvard agreed, holding Ria's gaze with a serious light in his blue eyes. "I've pledged to aid her in whatever way I can, and I've got the personnel to back that promise up. I don't want you to worry."

"Understood, sir. I know we'll all feel better knowing that she's in such good hands," the usually taciturn Dorian replied. It was obvious to Ria that her Guard had a history with Edvard. From the comments going back and forth, she figured Edvard had had some hand in Dorian's combat training.

"Now what about the rest of the team?" Ria asked, bringing the conversation back around to what she really wanted to know.

"Bronson went down hard. He's got injuries to both legs, broken ribs, a punctured lung, and possible concussion. The healer's with him now, but she says he'll survive. He's taking the treatment well and is already out of danger, though he'll be laid up for a while, recovering."

"Praise the Lady," Ria breathed, both appalled at the extent of the young man's injuries and glad that he was being cared for and would pull through. "What about the others?"

"Just minor injuries. We're all fine. When can we rejoin you?" Dorian sounded eager to get back to his job.

"Um…" Ria looked around at Jake and Edvard, not sure what to say.

"Dorian, is it?" Jake asked rhetorically, breaking into the conversation. "My name is Jake. Ben is a friend of mine," he explained. "Right now, we're good. We have some planning to do and arrangements to make. When we get back to a place where you can meet up with us, we'll call you in. Keep your team ready and alert the others of your kind. When the time comes, we'll need your support and we'll probably need it fast."

"Milady?" Dorian asked, putting all his unwillingness to listen to anyone but the Nyx into his tone.

"He's been right about everything so far, Dor. I think we'd better listen to him on this one." She knew that was equivalent to giving Jake an unmitigated endorsement. Dorian would understand that as well.

"Are you the seer, Jake?" Dorian asked, still sounding a bit skeptical.

Jake chuckled. "Yeah, though I usually don't go around advertising my abilities."

"What Clan are you?" Dorian demanded, warming a bit.

"No Clan. No Tribe. No Pack. I'm human," Jake admitted.

"Mage?" All of Dorian's outrage came through in that single word.

"Not quite. Just a seer. No other magic. I don't hang around with magic users. They make me itch. Mostly, I keep to myself, though I have connections to many different groups of shifters," Jake explained.

"I can vouch for him," Edvard said unexpectedly. "My nephew counts him as a dear friend and trusted ally."

That was news to Ria, though she supposed it shouldn't

have been. Jake had managed to get Sam to loan him his yacht and crew after all. Sam Kinkaid wasn't a pushover by any means. If he trusted Jake enough to loan out his yacht, his Uncle Ed, a platoon of selkies and who knew how many other shifters, then that really *meant* something.

"And his sister is Cade's mate," Ria put in, knowing her Guard knew and respected Cade's human mate. She had more than proved her worth—and her loyalties.

Everyone in her Guard knew Cade. He had been one of their most respected members until recently. He had retired from active duty when he found his mate.

Dorian kept quiet for a moment, foregoing the rest of his questions. Ria was glad. They had more important things to discuss.

They ended the call a short time later and resumed their dinner at a more leisurely pace. Ria's initial hunger had been addressed and she was able to enjoy her dessert as the men talked about the weather forecast for the next few days. Being on a boat in the middle of the Atlantic Ocean, the weather forecast was important to watch, and sure enough, a tropical depression was beginning to churn off the coast of Africa. It could pose a problem for the yacht in the next few days.

Ria started to feel tired. She'd had a long day, after all. Edvard noticed and the men ended their discussion. The big selkie gave her a hug before leaving her to Jake's guidance. It appeared Jake already knew his way around the ship—at least to the guest rooms—and was to be entrusted to escort her to the suite set aside for her use.

CHAPTER THREE

Jake walked Ria to her stateroom, seeing her to her door. He was very protective of her—like one of her Guards—but with a somewhat more intimate twist that was hard to define. But it was there, in his every gesture, in his words, even in his attitude toward her. He seemed to want to keep her safe for reasons known only to himself.

With her Guard, Ria knew why they risked their lives to keep her safe. She was the Nyx and there were generations of honor and duty standing between her position and the people who were sworn to keep the Nyx safe. They would have done the same for any Nyx. Not just her. Though she was sure most of them were very fond of her as a person, and she counted several of them as close friends. Some, like her cousin Cade, were even related to her, but none of them were there purely for her—just her, apart from her position. They were there for the Nyx, not Ria alone, but that was okay. Ria had become the Nyx, and the two were inseparable at this point. She just wished sometimes…that it could be different.

She wasn't sure where Jake stood on the matter, but she sensed his motivations for protecting her were much more complex. The vibes she was getting off him were more…personal, somehow. As if he would be there, helping her, regardless of whether or not she was the queen of her species. As if he actually cared about her as a person, irrespective of her function in shifter society and the sacred duty that haunted her.

"You'll be safe here for the night," Jake was saying as they drew closer to her door. "I doubt anyone or anything could get on this vessel without twenty shifters coming down hard on them, and the magical protections surrounding this yacht are the finest a selkie can spin, which is to say, very fine indeed." He smiled as they stopped in front of her door.

Jake didn't hesitate, but opened the door and walked in ahead of her—just as one of her Guard would have done—checking behind each possible place of concealment, including the attached bathroom. He nodded to her once he had checked every last inch of the place and she walked farther into the cabin, with what she knew was a bemused expression on her face.

She took the scrunchie out of her hair and tossed it on a small coffee table set between a sofa and a comfortable-looking chair. The room was big for a ship and had a sitting area in addition to the luxurious-looking bed. She ran her hands through her hair as she went over to the small, mirrored bar and opened a can of soda, pouring it into a glass. As an afterthought, she splashed a bit of rum into the glass along with some ice and took a sip as she turned around. She leaned against the bar, looking at Jake. He hadn't moved.

"Do you want a nightcap?" she asked in a quiet voice, slowly sipping her spiked soda.

"I'd better not." But he didn't move. His eyes followed her hand as she raised the glass to her lips and sipped at the cool, bubbly liquid.

She took her time, watching him just as closely. There was something in his eyes when he looked at her...something almost feral. Which was an odd thought, considering he wasn't a shifter.

"Why are you here, Jake?" Her tone was both soft and challenging.

He surprised her by stepping closer, coming very near her personal space. She didn't mind. There was something very soothing about his presence and he didn't frighten her. On the contrary, he intrigued her beyond all expectations. Who knew a human could be so compelling?

"I'm here for you, milady." His gaze held hers and she knew there was more to his words than their simple meaning.

She put her glass down on the tabletop behind her, the crystal clinking against the marble top of the bar. Her gaze never left his and something started to glow down deep inside her. A spark of attraction that had never quite been extinguished since the moment they had danced at that wedding all those months ago.

"There's more to it than that," she challenged. "You're not like the members of my Guard. I can't quite figure you out. What motivates you? Why do you look at me so differently than everyone else? You don't seem intimidated by my position in the least, which is something I'm not used to. Every shifter fears my power. Even humans shy away from me. And yet, here you are."

He moved right into her personal space then, standing directly in front of her, his hips aligned with hers, his warm body only inches from her. She had to tilt her head to meet his gaze and it felt good. Right.

"Here I am," he agreed. "I'm here for *you*, Ria." He repeated his earlier statement, emphasizing the words differently this time, making her breath catch. His eyes swirled with potent energy—a raw power that almost mesmerized her as his head dipped and his lips touched hers.

She was lost the moment he kissed her. Her eyes closed and she gave in to the sensation of his kiss, allowing herself to enjoy the feel of his firm mouth claiming her lips, her mouth, her tongue. His taste was welcome…almost familiar. He tasted like home. Like all that was good and right in the world. And then he put his arms around her and pulled her body into alignment with his.

She trembled as she felt his hard muscles shifting against

35

her body, his warmth, his human heat. He smelled divine and felt even better to her starved senses. It had been so long since she had been this close to a man. Any man. And she had never been so close to a human—even a human with magic of his own.

Jake's magic was of a different flavor than what she was used to. It wasn't aggressive. It wasn't scary in any way. It was comforting and accepting. Ancient and wise. Something about it called to her and made her feel at home with him.

This close, she could feel the tingle of his magic against her body. She had felt it before, when they had danced at the wedding, but it hadn't been nearly this potent. And with him kissing her, the magic shivered inside her as well. It felt good. Pure and hot and as male as she was female. Complimentary to her own rare form of magic and perfectly aligned. She felt her chest vibrate with sensation—with sound. Sweet Mother of All! She was purring in human form.

Something clicked inside her and she broke the kiss, staring up into his eyes.

Dear Goddess. She had just found her mate.

"Now do you understand?" Jake's gaze challenged her and she realized that somehow…he had known. Maybe he really was a seer.

"You knew?"

"Honey, did you doubt my abilities?" He read the truth in her eyes. "You did." He seemed defeated with those two little words. He sighed as he rested his forehead against hers. He just held her for a few moments, saying nothing, until finally he let her go and moved away.

He didn't go far. Just a foot to the side, where he could reach the bottle of hundred-year-old Scotch that stood on the bar. He poured himself a few fingers and swigged it back, savoring for a moment, before turning to face her again.

"I guess I shouldn't be surprised. I've had time to get used to the idea. You've only just discovered it. I didn't mean to rush you or imply that I was disappointed. I know it's got to take some getting used to for a shifter—especially a monarch—to find their destiny with a mere human."

"You're not a *mere* anything," she objected. "Your magic tingles against mine. You're powerful in your own right and if that little demonstration was anything to go by, magically, we seem pretty evenly matched. You might even have a bit more than I do, which I find…intriguing."

He moved closer once again, reaching out to wrap his hands around her waist and pull her closer. She liked the little show of dominance. Her inner cat especially appreciated the male animal that dared touch her so familiarly. Nobody had *ever* dared such a bold thing without serious danger of getting their eyes scratched out, but the cat liked this man. Even if he was only human. There was something about his magic that stroked the cat's fur in just the right way.

And wasn't that surprising?

Her cat had never liked being touched by males. It had put up with a few in the past, but it had never welcomed one the way it welcomed Jake. It *liked* him.

No, it was way more than mere liking. It loved the way he made the cat purr.

"I've been waiting for you for a long time, Ria," he said in a low, seductive tone that shivered through her. "I've been seeing you in my visions for years now."

"Years, huh?" she was both impressed and breathless. She had never expected to find her mate in such a way, but she knew shifters often knew the moment they met their perfect match. "I knew there was something different about you at the wedding, but we didn't get much time alone. I've thought about you a lot since then, though. A lot more than I should have been thinking about a human I'd met only once. I probably should have realized you were something special."

She leaned in, placing her ear over his heart, allowing herself to soak in the feel of his strength, and the warm scent of his embrace. He felt so good. And his heart beat a steady, reassuring rhythm against her ear.

"You thought about me?" She heard the uncertainty in his voice and was warmed by it. He might be a seer, but he didn't know everything, it seemed. She smiled.

"Yeah, I did. Did you think about me?" Her voice dropped low, the cat's purr breaking through. It had never done that before, but she recognized the sign for what it was. The cat wanted its mate. For that matter, so did Ria. Only, her human half was feeling a bit shy.

He was human. What if he didn't understand what mating meant among her kind? Sure his sister was mated to her cousin, but how much had Ellie told him about shifter mating? Did Jake understand what it meant to her? Was he taking this as seriously as she was?

So many questions jumbled through her mind, but it all came back to one thing. Jake was her mate and she was in his arms. Where she belonged. The cat understood it on the most basic level and her human heart, though scared, felt the same. She prayed to the Goddess that he would realize the import of what they were to each other in time, if he didn't understand it already.

"I've dreamed of you waking and sleeping, Ria."

Now that sounded promising. She began to take heart. Maybe he did understand, after all.

"You're my mate, Jake," she whispered. "Do you understand what that means?"

He drew back, lifting away so he could meet her gaze once more. "Not completely, but I promise to spend the rest of my life trying to figure it out." He smiled and she felt a lightness fill her heart.

"The rest of your life, huh?" She reached up, cupping his cheeks, then moving her hands around to draw his head down toward hers. "I really like the sound of that," she whispered against his lips. "Mating is forever, Jake. Now that I have you, I'll never let you go."

"I'll hold you to that, milady," he replied before taking her lips with his again.

His kiss this time was spiced with the bite of the Scotch he had drunk. She liked it on him, though she didn't generally enjoy the flavor of hard liquor. Mixed with Jake, though, it tasted divine. Of course, that could just be Jake.

She wanted to get closer. She wanted...to get naked with him and spend the rest of the night learning all about how her mate made love. Was it too soon?

Among shifters, it wouldn't be. It was natural for mates to come together as soon as they recognized each other and stay together for a lifetime thereafter. There was no doubt when two shifters mated. At least, not in the normal course of things.

But Jake was human. Magical, to be sure, but still human. That skewed the equation.

Didn't it?

Jake didn't seem to care. He took the kiss deeper, wrapping his arms around her and moving toward the bed on the far side of the room. She didn't object. In fact, she helped as best she could while under the drugging influence of his kiss. He touched her skin, revealing it with hasty actions, tugging on her clothes and pulling on zippers and buttons that blocked his path.

She broke away briefly to do the same for him, but she didn't get very far. Before she knew it, she was naked and he was only partly so. His chest was heavily muscled and full of interesting contours she wanted to explore with her fingers...and her tongue. But he was driving her wild and she couldn't really concentrate when he broke the kiss and lowered his mouth to her neck, then lower.

When his lips closed over the tight point of her breast, she nearly screeched in satisfaction. She held onto his head, running her fingers through his silky hair in approval. He seemed to know just how to touch her, using the perfect amount of pressure wherever their skin met.

He turned to lower her to the bed and she didn't want to let him go. Not even for a moment, but she also wanted his pants gone. If they weren't gone soon, the cat might come out and shred the fabric, but Ria tried to calm her animal instincts. She didn't want to scare him off. Not when things were just about to get really interesting.

She focused instead on finding the button and zipper of his pants, sliding it down while he was bent over her body, his strong arms caging her torso as his lips tasted hers again. She strained to push his pants down over his hip, glad when she could feel skin under her fingertips.

She wanted more.

Purring almost non-stop, she turned the tables on her mate, rolling them both so that she was on top. Jake didn't resist. In fact, he smiled, his eyes flashing hot when she took him by surprise. He liked that she let her inner sex kitten out to play. Until him, she didn't know she even had one.

The cat was hot and wanted him now. No more waiting. The woman allowed him only a moment to catch his breath before she climbed over him and impaled her wet pussy on his hard cock. Oh yeah, that's what she wanted. Both the woman and the cat that lived inside her took a moment to savor the first feel of her mate.

Her hair fell around them as she bent down over him and held his gaze as she began to move. A slow sensual glide made her ultra-aware of every last inch of her mate. He fit her so well, she was panting already, her body rocketing into places she had never been before. It seemed she had been waiting for the right man all these years and finally—finally—she had found him. Or he had found her. It didn't really matter at the moment, while they were as close as two people could be.

And still, she wanted to be closer. She began to rock on his hardness, allowing her body to take control where her mind left off. Thinking was overrated anyway. Feeling...now *that* was the right thing to do in this situation. Her hunky mate hard and ready and filling her to overflowing, her body feeling languid and tense all at the same time, her senses reeling into places that were delicious and unfamiliar. Yeah, this was the time to let go of the thinking part and just feel.

She sat up, riding him hard now, running her fingers over his hard-muscled chest. He had the most wonderful build. He was honed. Like a hunting cat. Or an athlete. Her more primitive side approved. She wanted to lick him all over. But that would come later.

Right now, she needed to come, like she needed her next breath. She needed the relief that only being with her mate could give. And she needed it now. She sped her pace, glad when his strong hands went to her hips, helping guide her and taking some of the strain off her leg muscles. She wasn't used to riding like this, but something told her it would become a common occurrence with Jake in her life now.

She looked forward to training her thighs every chance she got. Ria smiled as her head dropped back on her shoulders, instinct taking over as her body began to quake. Her inner muscles clenched hard around him and she could feel an answering tightness in his body. She screeched as she came, his groan sounding only a moment later as his warm come filled her quivering channel.

She rode him through the shared orgasm, slowing and finally coming to a rest, draping her body over his as they both caught their breath.

"Jake?" She pet his chest, content to lie in his arms as they both quieted.

"Mmm," he replied, the lazy sound sending new shivers down her spine.

But she couldn't give in to the satisfied lethargy threatening to claim her. She had serious things to discuss with him. Life-altering things.

She lifted up a bit so she could look into his eyes.

"Jake?" she asked again. His eyes opened and gazed up into hers. The look on his face was one of joy and satisfaction, mirroring what she was feeling too—except for the trepidation about what she had to say next. She decided to just get it all out. Like ripping off a bandage, it was probably better to do this quickly. "Jake, I was serious before. I just want to make sure you know that. You're my mate."

She watched his expression carefully as a broad smile came over his lips and he tugged her a little closer.

"I like the sound of that even better now that I know how

great we are together." He kissed her temple in a playful move, but she was trying to be serious.

"Mating means something really important among shifters, Jake." She tried to make him understand, but he was still being a little more flippant than she wished.

"If it means we get to do this every day for the rest of our lives, I'm all for it."

Hope lifted her heart a tiny bit. He was thinking in terms of forever, but was he only teasing? Mating was deadly serious among her kind.

"The rest of our lives," she repeated his words more slowly. "That's what mating means, Jake. Are you up for *that?*" She wasn't smiling now. No, she was challenging him to match her serious mood.

His expression turned grave and her heart sank. Had she scared him off? Had she overdone it? But, dammit, she had a right to know what he was thinking. He was her *mate*. There were no secrets among mates. Her inner cat protested the very idea that he could be thinking in less permanent terms about their relationship.

Jake sat up in the bed, taking her with him until they faced each other. He slid his hands down over her arms until he could grasp both of her hands with his.

"I am very serious when I say that I am with you for the duration. As long as you'll have me, Ria," he said in a deep, somber tone, his gaze searching hers. "I have an inkling what mating means for your people, but not being a shifter myself, all I can say is that I've seen us together when we're old and gray, and our joy in each other never diminishes. I want that. I want that future with you, sweetheart. Of all the possibilities I've ever foreseen, that's the thing I want the most. You. In my life. For the rest of my life. Is that enough for your inner cat? Will you be satisfied with that?"

It was on the tip of her tongue to demand one thing more, but she figured she'd gotten enough out of him for now. It was early days in their relationship and he was already thinking in terms of forever—which satisfied her cat very well indeed.

The human part of her wanted his heart as well, but she figured that would come in time. They were on the same page. It would just take a bit of time and shared experiences to cement the relationship into what she wanted most…his love.

Near the empty warehouse on the shores of North Carolina, Master Willard Fontanbleu, Necromancer of the *Venifucus* Council of Elders seethed. His scraggly, long gray beard whipped around his portly body as he chastised those who worked for him.

"You let her escape!" A little bit of spittle shot out of his mouth along with the words. He was in a frothing rage. "She was within your grasp and you let her escape!"

"My lord, she had a team of commandos on the roof with a Blackhawk. There was no way we could have known she had such resources at her disposal. Our intelligence didn't prepare us properly for such resistance." The man was just a little too belligerent for Willard's liking, but that would soon be remedied—or Willard would have a new commander of his small army. "My lord, we simply didn't think—"

"Think?" Willard cut him off, tired of his bleating. "I'm not paying you to think, damn you! I'm paying you to apprehend the woman. No more, no less. So far, all you've given me is excuses." Willard stared the man down. The soldier might be bigger and more physically fit than Willard, but he knew nothing of real power. Willard let the fire of his magic flare in his eyes and was gratified when the soldier involuntarily moved back a step. "You will get her next time or you will die trying. Understood?" The soldier gulped visibly and Willard finally had reason to smile. It wasn't a pleasant smile for those viewing it, he realized, but it made him feel better to know his people grasped the lengths to which he would go to get his way. "You're dismissed."

Willard turned his back on the man, adding insult to the verbal injury he'd just inflicted. If the soldier was a little better at his job, Willard might've thought twice about showing his back to the man, but as it was, they both knew now who was the stronger one in this relationship.

Willard motioned for his aide to approach. The little toady annoyed the shit out of him mostly, but he was useful—even if he was a spy for the Council. Aaron came up alongside Willard and immediately began his usual, unctuous speech.

"What may I do to assist you, my lord?"

Aaron was a total suck up, but that's what Willard wanted right now. Someone who wouldn't argue with him and would do whatever he said—exactly what he said. Even if Aaron was filing regular reports with his detractors on the Council, Willard didn't mind right now. Not when he was so close to achieving his goal.

"I want you to go back to the warehouse and trace the energy patterns. Find out where the Royal Guard slunk away to, and see if you can get a better bead on where the Nyx went, if you can. Then report back to me—and me alone. Understand?" Willard made eye contact, hoping to impress his will upon his aide though he knew Aaron had other, undisclosed masters.

"Yes, my lord. It will be done immediately." Aaron actually bowed his way out of Willard's presence. It was one of the quirky little things that made Willard smile and was probably the reason he continued to allow Aaron to live. He was amusing for a worm.

But Aaron, and everyone else in the organization, didn't really understand why Willard was so obsessed with the *pantera* Nyx. He wasn't about to explain it to them either. He knew a secret about the Nyx's power. A secret he was not going to share with anyone until he was good and ready.

He'd be ready when he had the Nyx's power for his own. Though…he might not tell anyone even then. After all, they laughed at him when he claimed to be a true necromancer. He had only communicated with the dead once—and that had been mostly by accident. A real necromancer—a mage who could raise the dead—hadn't been seen in the mortal realm in centuries. Nowadays, the term was merely one of the many ceremonial titles applied to various positions on the Council of Elders.

Willard couldn't raise the dead. He couldn't even establish a reliable intuitive connection like a paltry psychic medium. He might have the ancient title of Necromancer of the Council of Elders, but it wasn't a true designation of his magic. He was powerful, but his talents lay more in elemental matters, not necromancy.

But with the Nyx's power—then he could very well become an actual necromancer. He could use her power for his own, and nobody would ever need to know. Killing her and taking her gift would improve his situation within Council by leaps and bounds. Which was why he continued to try to capture the woman—no matter how many times she slithered through his fingers.

He would get her one of these days...no matter how long it took him.

CHAPTER FOUR

Jake woke with a start a couple of hours later. They had made spectacular love once more and then settled into an exhausted, well-satisfied sleep—only to be disturbed by the visions that never quite let him go. This one had been a doozy.

He sat up in bed and realized Ria was awake beside him. He scrubbed at his face with one hand, even as he reached for his phone, forgetting for a second that it wouldn't work all the way out here at sea.

"Damn." He got out of bed, knowing he had to reach the communications center on the bridge as soon as possible. He had to warn—

"What is it?" Ria asked, already up and throwing on some clothes as he did the same.

"Vision," he answered in a clipped voice, before he could stop himself. He felt bad instantly. Ria deserved better than a one-word answer. "Sorry. I had a vision. It happens sometimes, in my sleep. It can be disorienting." He apologized as he stepped into his pants, dressing as quickly as he could. He didn't bother with the shirt, pausing only to step into his boots before arming himself and heading for the door.

He paused for just a moment, surprised to see Ria right

behind him. She had dressed quickly and silently, ready to assist. In that moment, he realized he couldn't love her more. She didn't even know what was going on, but she was ready to help him, no matter what. Having a mate was going to take some getting used to. Jake had been on his own with his talent for so long. It would be nice to have someone else to depend on when the more disruptive visions hit.

They would have to have a long talk about what happened to him when the really big ones struck him. He wanted her to be prepared before it happened, in case she was with him at the time. And judging by her willingness to follow him into who-knew-what, she probably would be. It would take time to readjust his thinking, but he looked forward to having a partner in life now in a way he had never anticipated before.

He opened the door, a smile on his face despite the situation. "I have to get to the comm center. I have to call Ben and warn him. The guys who tried to take you earlier are going to try to kidnap one or more of your Guards, hoping to use them to get to you. They think your Guards either know where you are or can be used to force you out of hiding."

He heard her gasp, but other than that small reaction, she was right beside him as they climbed up through the ship toward the bridge. It was the middle of the night, but Jake noted a number of dark shapes skulking in the darkness, observing their path. No doubt the crew on the bridge knew they were on their way already and would be waiting for them when they got there.

Jake thought it was interesting that nobody seemed in any mood to stop them and question why they were prowling around the ship in the middle of the night. All they had to do was take one look at Jake to know he'd been in a hurry. He wasn't wearing a shirt, for one thing, his pants were just barely fastened, and his boot laces weren't tied. It would be obvious to anyone looking at him that he had dressed in a hurry. He liked the fact that Edvard had apparently given Jake the run of the ship—instructing his people not to interfere. That level of trust was something he hadn't expected and greatly valued.

"Did you see anything about when this might be happening?" Ria asked, still keeping pace with him. She was as silent as her cat and an excellent companion. Jake realized he couldn't have asked for a better match. Ria was everything he had never dared hope for in a woman—and he knew he had only just scratched the surface on getting to know her.

"It was daylight. Angle of the sun looked like afternoon. They have a few hours yet to prepare, and maybe turn the tables on their attackers," he replied, climbing the last set of stairs toward their goal.

Surprisingly, Edvard himself was on the bridge when they got there. His hair was wet and he was wearing a terrycloth robe, a towel in his hand that had in all likelihood just been rubbed over his hair, which was standing out at odd angles.

Ria sniffed and grinned. "Did we interrupt your dip in the ocean, Uncle Ed?"

As they got closer to the ship's captain, even Jake could smell the brine of the seawater that clung to Edvard. No doubt the seal shifter had just hopped out of the water.

"A wee fishie told me you looked like you were in a hurry," Ed said without apology. "Is there something I can help you with?"

"I need to get a message to my man on the shore," Jake replied, unsmiling. "They're in danger."

Ed led the way to the comm console, punching up a few different screens before turning over the interface to Jake. He didn't waste any time inputting the number for Ben's cell phone. Thankfully, the call was answered on the second ring. Ben didn't sound sleepy, which meant he'd been standing watch.

"Ben, it's Jake. You've got to move your guests. Your position will be compromised by this afternoon. Best not leave anything there for them to remember you by."

"Any ideas where we should bug out to?" Ben asked. Jake was glad his human friend understood him enough by now not to question his intel. Instead, he asked the right question—what environment wouldn't match what Jake had seen in his vision.

"Stay away from the beach and flatlands. I suggest the woods or better yet, the mountains. Head west. Remember the site we discussed out that way?"

"Affirmative," Ben answered, all business now. "We can be on our way in a half hour. Is that soon enough?"

"Should be," Jake answered, already breathing easier. "As long as you clear the flatlands before noon. Get your asses into the woods."

"Heard and understood, Major. Do you want a check-in when we get there?"

"That'd probably be best," Jake replied, looking up to meet Ria's gaze. Everybody on the bridge heard the conversation, but Jake didn't mind. He was firmly in the presence of allies—something that was usually a rarity in his line of work. "While I have you, can you give me an update?"

"Sure thing," Ben agreed affably. "These cats heal quick. The youngster is able to walk, which is a goddamn miracle, if you ask me. He's moving slow, but he's moving under his own steam and the healer says he'll be good as new in a few days."

"That's a relief to hear. So everyone is up and able to evac?" he asked, just to be clear. He could see Ria was eager for any word on her people.

"Oh yeah," Ben answered. "There's no holding these folks back. They're impatient to be off and out to get a little of their own back. They're mad more than anything else. And kind of appalled that a mere human is doing their job." Ben laughed and Jake had to smile in response.

"I bet. Just tell them to sit tight. They'll have ample opportunity to bloody their claws before this is over. That's a guarantee."

Jake looked over at Ria, raising one eyebrow in silent question. If she had any further questions, he was giving her an opportunity to ask them. She shook her head and Jake ended the call with a few final words to his friend, Ben.

When he disconnected, he sat back, sighing heavily. He contemplated the console for a moment, trying to gather his wits from the early morning vision. He was still a little disoriented, but having Ria's steady presence at his side helped in ways he never would have expected.

"You okay, son?" Edvard's deep voice cut through the fog that still surrounded Jake's mind.

Jake looked up at the older man. "Yeah. I'm getting there. Sorry. This one was a little intense."

Edvard put one beefy hand on Jake's shoulder. "It's always worse when they hit during sleep. Or so my sister claims. I've seen her stumble around in a fog for an hour or two after waking from a vision more than once. She was a seer from an early age, as I think, were you."

Jake nodded, not seeing any reason to hide the fact that he had come to his talent young. He stood and immediately, Ria was at his side. Edvard watched them with a calculating grin as he moved back enough to let them pass.

"Since we're all up, can I invite you to join me for breakfast? Or maybe a bracing dip in the ocean?" Edvard asked, a teasing light in his eyes.

"Looks like you've already been in the water," Ria observed as they walked toward the door that led off the bridge. "But if it's safe, I'd love to give it a go." She looked at Jake, challenge in her gaze that he couldn't ignore. Seemed his lady had a spirit of adventure that had been kept under wraps until now.

Jake pushed the door open and looked downward toward the dark water far below. Dawn hadn't quite started yet and the early morning air was dark and mysterious. One of his favorite times of day. He checked his pockets for anything that wouldn't handle a dunking, toeing off his boots. He was glad he had chosen to arm himself with a knife rather than a firearm when he'd left the stateroom earlier.

"You—or your people in the water—won't mind if I dive from here, will you?" Jake asked, sensing it was time to demonstrate a little of his abilities. He might be human, but he'd trained hard to be able to keep up with most shifters. He might not be able to outswim a selkie, but he definitely could put on a show that might earn a little bit of respect.

Edvard looked at him with a measuring gaze. "No need to prove anything to me, lad. There's a perfectly good platform for diving a few decks down."

"And I hope you'll escort Ria there," Jake replied, moving his boots out of the way as he climbed up on the rail that ringed the bridge. He was on the side of the ship and the drop was substantial to the water, but doable. "I know many of your people are wondering who I am and what gives me the right to be here. Actions speak louder than words, in my experience. Plus, right now, the water is just what I need to clear my head."

Without further ado, he dove.

It might not be the smartest thing he'd ever done, but his emotions had been running high since being with Ria. She had quite literally blown his mind. His emotional equilibrium was shot to hell, but he didn't really mind. He knew he had to get a grip—and soon—for the sake of their mission, but a part of him wanted to revel in the storm of feeling that rushed through him each time he took Ria in his arms. Hell, it happened every time she even just looked at him in that certain way she had. He was a goner and he didn't mind at all.

Jake parted the water with barely a ripple and he was proud of the dive he'd just executed. He might not win any gold medals at the Olympics, but he knew that near-silent high dive had probably scored points with the selkies on that giant boat. And those in the water beside him.

Jake circled upward and headed for the surface. He popped up the way he'd gone in, with as little sound as possible, unsurprised to find a trio of selkies in seal form swimming in a loose circle around him. They checked him out for a moment or two, then moved off to a slight distance, keeping him within the perimeter they'd set up around the anchored ship.

A splash to his right made him look. Sure enough, Ria—

clad in a lovely turquoise bikini she must've borrowed from the ship's stores—was entering the water from a much lower diving platform. He propelled himself in her direction, wanting to keep her in his sights while she was in the water. They were surrounded by some of the best and most magical swimmers in the world, who were thankfully, on their side, but something inside him demanded that Jake keep his new mate in his sight whenever the slightest danger presented itself.

He realized right away that she was a strong swimmer. She might not be the diver he had worked to become, but she was at home in the water. She swam over to him and splashed him playfully.

"Jake!" Her low tone was chastising, but filled with humor at the same time. "Don't ever scare me like that again. I didn't know you were part fish."

"Well, now you do." He swam around her, teasing her as she turned to keep him in sight. "I worked very hard to learn how to dive, and I enjoy a chance to show off in front of my girl now and again. You don't begrudge me that, surely? Don't shifter males show off for their mates?"

"Not by scaring them. Not if they want to keep their bits in the proper places." She reached out and dug her fingernails—which were just a tiny bit sharper and a lot stronger than they would be on a human woman—into his shoulders. Her leg slid between his and he had to suppress a growl.

"I like my bits exactly where they are," he replied to her teasing, both verbal and physical. The cold, ocean water made not one bit of difference when he had Ria in his arms. She turned him on like a lightning bolt.

"Mmm." She rubbed closer, sliding against his body, heating the water in their vicinity. He wouldn't be surprised to see steam rising around them. "I do too."

"Come now, children," Edvard's voice cut through the pre-dawn ocean stillness. The selkie—in human form—had come up behind them silently. "I thought we were going to swim, not cuddle."

Ria sighed loudly. "Okay. How about a lap around the yacht?"

Edvard looked at Ria doubtfully, then moved to assess Jake. "Do you think you can both handle that?"

Ria shrugged as Jake nodded. "If I get tired, I'll depend on one of you to fish me out," Ria joked, clearly not ashamed to admit that she might not be able to keep up with a selkie in the ocean.

Jake had a little more pride, but he would've admitted it if the trek around the huge ship was going to be a problem. He knew he could make it and between him and Edvard—and all the shifters in the water around them—they would keep an eye on Ria.

Jake met Edvard's gaze over Ria's head, nodding once more. "We'll go slow. A nice, leisurely morning exercise swim," Jake said, knowing by the challenging light in Ria's eyes that she wasn't going to do any such thing.

She turned and splashed away. The race was on.

Ria loved the cool water and the vastness of the ocean. It was refreshing after being cooped up inside for the past day. She was used to moving and stretching her legs. Activity was second nature to a shifter and she had been idle too long.

She didn't usually get much chance to swim—especially not in the ocean—so she enjoyed setting as fast a pace as she could manage around the big yacht. She had expected Edvard to keep pace with her easily, but Jake surprised her not only with his stamina, but his speed. He was a better swimmer than she was, hands down. Her human mate was full of surprises.

When they lapped the boat and came back to the low platform where she had entered the water, she made for the ladder, winded. Jake wasn't even breathing hard. And of course, Edvard waited only until she climbed out to do a spectacular backwards leap away, diving under the water and staying down so long, she lost track of him as she collected a robe and toweled her hair.

"I wonder if they have a dryer on this tub?" Jake asked, struggling out of his wet jeans at her side. He had put on the big robe that had been waiting for him. There were several of the big, fluffy garments hanging ready for people to hop out of the ocean.

"I suspect there's every comfort of home on this vessel," she replied, bending to help him by grabbing the end of one leg of his jeans as he hopped, struggling with the wet fabric.

As they moved to one side of the wide platform, a seal bounded out of the ocean next to them, transforming as it went, into a man. A sleekly muscled, very good looking man. And he was naked...and very well endowed. Ria couldn't help but notice before the man reached for a robe and hid his...uh...assets...from view.

"Son of a gun," Jake swore, but there was a broad smile on his face. "I should've known." He stepped forward to meet the man, his hand outstretched. "Tom Kinkaid as I live and breathe."

The two men shook hands and included a back slapping bro-hug in their repertoire of greeting. It was the friendliest greeting Ria had seen Jake give anyone so far. This guy had to be a good friend—or at least, one Jake hadn't seen in a long time.

"I thought that was you doing the swan dive off the bridge deck. Trying to impress Uncle Ed?" Tom asked, grinning from ear to ear.

If anything, the smile made the man even more handsome as a dimple appeared on one cheek. It was a good thing Ria had found her mate, or she'd have been in mortal danger of falling in serious *like* with the handsome selkie.

"Not sure anything impresses the old man," Jake answered with a rueful expression. "But I figured it couldn't hurt to try. I'm feeling at a decided disadvantage around all your people. Hell, Tom. I had no idea you were one of *those* Kinkaids."

"And I had no idea you knew about us. Damn, Jake. Too many secrets." Tom shook his head as Jake stepped back to include Ria into their small circle.

"You can say that again. Ria, honey," Jake said, putting a possessive arm around her waist as he drew her into the conversation. "This is Tom Kinkaid, the dive master who taught me everything I know about diving, both with gear and off the high diving board."

"Ma'am," Tom nodded to Ria respectfully, his gaze taking in the way she fit against Jake. Yeah, she saw the moment he figured out they were together. "I never realized the major here was mated into a Clan."

"He wasn't," Ria replied honestly. "Not until just recently, though his sister mated my cousin a few months back. He's known about us for a while." She reached out to shake the man's hand. "Why do you call him Major?" She realized that was the second time she'd heard Jake referred to by that term. Was it a rank? Had he been a soldier? It made sense. He certainly had all kinds of military skills and training.

Tom seemed confused for a moment as he looked from Jake to Ria and back again. "Uh…"

"I was a major in the Marines. Force Recon. Special Operations. I did a little training with the SEALs—though I didn't realize at the time that you guys really were seals."

Tom shrugged. "We like the irony."

Ria laughed. "Our mating is very new," she explained, knowing the selkie was still confused about why she hadn't known about Jake's background.

"Congratulations are in order, then," Tom smiled. "Will I see you both at breakfast? I'd love a chance to catch up a bit, now that Jake knows what we are."

"Edvard invited us to breakfast after our swim but he's still in the water," Ria looked back over the dark ocean, the dawn just barely beginning to kiss the sky to the east.

"He's giving you time to shower and change. Go up to your rooms, get the salt off your skin and I'll see you in the breakfast room. I can send someone to show you the way if you don't know the lay of the ship yet," Tom offered.

Ria looked to Jake, but he shrugged. "I guess we could use

that guide. I haven't seen the breakfast room yet."

"All right. How about a half hour? Is that enough time? I'll send my sister to get you. She's got too much spare time on her hands as it is," Tom joked.

"Sounds like a plan," Ria answered. "Now which way was our cabin?"

Tom took pity and showed them the way to the guest cabins, chatting a bit with Jake as they went along. He showed them parts of the ship they hadn't yet seen and talked about how the salt water didn't bother selkie skin the way it did other shifters and humans.

It seemed as though he was enjoying the ability to speak freely about what he was with Jake for the first time. It was clear the two men respected each other and had a deep-seated friendship.

They were almost to the cabin when Jake stopped short. Ria looked at him, touching his arm as she looked into his eyes. Power swirled there, making her gasp. His eyes were fixed straight ahead as he stood stock still in the middle of the companionway.

Tom looked back, halting as his affable smile disappeared by slow degrees. "What's wrong with him?"

"I'm not sure, but I think he's having a vision."

"Sweet Mother of All," the selkie swore. "A vision? He's a seer? A mage?"

"A seer, yes. Not a mage. Not exactly," she answered absently, worried about Jake as he just stood there. "Or so he says."

"I always knew there was powerful magic around him, but I had no idea it was...this." Tom looked both appalled and kind of reverent. "Let me get Ed. He'll know what to do." Tom ran ahead to the junction of the companionway where an intercom was tucked discretely into the wall. Ria heard him connect with the bridge quietly while she held Jake's hand and watched him, worrying.

Edvard came up behind them a moment later, but Jake hadn't moved. He took in the situation quickly and began barking questions.

"How long has he been like this?" Ed bit out, taking Jake's other hand and feeling for his pulse.

Tom looked at his watch. "About a minute and a half."

"Damn," Edvard cursed. "A powerful one, then. But he's got a lot of personal energy. His pulse is erratic but strong."

"What can we do to help him?" Ria asked in a small voice, not willing to disturb her mate. She didn't know what loud noises would do to his state.

"You're doing it," Edvard replied in a similarly gentle tone. "Protect his body while his mind is in the otherworlds. Be there for him when he comes out of it. Hold his hand. Be ready in case he needs you," Edvard ticked off his list as he let go of Jake's wrist and placed his arm down gently at his side. "Just do what you're doing. It is all we, who do not share his burden, can do. He'll come out of it on his own, once the vision has had its way with him."

"Are you sure?" Ria asked, still scared for her new mate. The cat inside her was clawing to get out, wanting to protect its mate from whatever threatened him.

"I've seen this before, with my sister. So far, she has always come out of this state on her own, but there are dangers." Edvard was as brutally honest as she expected him to be. She valued that about him.

"What dangers?" she demanded quietly.

"There are tales of seers falling into fugue states from which they never awaken," he said quietly, his voice kept low, but strong. "But Jake is made of stronger stuff than that. I have no doubt he knows how to handle these things. From what I have learned, he has carried this burden since he was very young, just like my sister. When it comes to them young, the power is greater, but so is the control over their abilities. Or so my sister's teachers always claimed."

"I don't even know if Jake had teachers for his gift or if he learned how to use it all on his own. There aren't a lot of humans running around with this amount of magic who aren't full-out mages, and Jake said he didn't like being around mages. He said they make his skin itch," she told Edvard, rubbing her thumb over Jake's knuckles, feeling the warmth of his skin.

"Sneeze too." Jake's voice was weak, but there. When she looked quickly up into his eyes, the power had stopped swirling in their depths. He was back. Mostly.

"What?" His words made no sense.

"Mages make me sneeze too," he clarified, his voice growing stronger as he seemed to regain his grip on the waking world. "Sorry. Was I standing here long?" He shook his head, looking around him as if to assess where he was. He was definitely disoriented. Like he had been earlier that morning, only worse.

"A little over five minutes," Tom reported, looking at his watch. "You back with us, Major?"

Jake shook his head from side to side, as if to clear it. "Yeah, I'm with you. Damn. That was a long one. Sorry."

"Don't apologize for your power," Edvard intoned as Jake bent over and put his hands on his knees. Ria stood protectively at his side, watching him carefully to see if there was anything she could do to help him. Jake looked up at Edvard as his eyes continued to clear.

"We have to get back to land," Jake said. His tone was urgent. "By tomorrow at the very latest. By tomorrow night the water will not be safe. Not with what they're calling up from the depths. Gather your people, Ed. No one will be safe in the water after tonight."

"Can we stop it?" Tom asked, his eyes narrowing in concern.

"No. I'm sorry. This isn't your battle, but there are those who will make the waters safe again. Not selkies. Something else. Something very magical and…you know them. They're soldiers, but they're not like you. Not exactly." Jake shook his head again. "Sorry, it's not clear. You might help them when they come, but this battle is theirs. And it won't be for a while yet. Until then, keep your people safely ashore. You do *not* want any of them to run afoul of this thing, believe me."

"What is it?" Ria asked the question she was sure they all wanted to ask.

"I don't know what you call it, but it's evil. Pure evil. A servant of the Destroyer from ancient times. Elspeth considered it a pet. I saw that much. It was defeated the last time only with the loss of many lives and sent to sleep for centuries. Elspeth's servants in the *Venifucus* are waking it up even as we speak and this is one seriously bad thing we cannot stop. Anyone who tries will die needlessly. Ed," Jake looked directly at the ship's captain, "please confirm that with your sister. She'll be calling shortly, I think. I wasn't alone on the psychic plane. Many seers just saw what I did. Or at least, parts of it. Damn." Jake put his head down again and breathed hard while Ria stroked his back, seeking to comfort him. "That was a doozy."

Aaron, the toad, had found where the Royal Guard had fallen back to lick their wounds, but they were gone again before Willard could mobilize his strike team to finish them off. Aaron was working on finding them again while Willard answered a call from the Council.

A great magical Work was in progress and ready to be unleashed, but they needed Willard's particular elemental talents to make it happen. They might ridicule him and his little obsession with the *pantera* Nyx, but they still needed him.

There was a reason Willard had been able to join the Council and maintain that position for many years, despite the constant challenges and derision of the other Council members. Willard was very good with water. It was his element, you might say. He had certain abilities with the water and its creatures that made him valuable to the Council, and they were calling on him now, to aid one of their little plans.

While he thought they were going about bringing Elspeth—the *Mater Priori*—back from the farthest realm all wrong, he didn't want to share his wisdom or intel about the Nyx with any of those selfish creatures that populated the Council. Willard lived with the comfort that when he made it possible for Elspeth to cross the barrier between the forgotten realms and this mortal one, she would reward him beyond reckoning. And wouldn't the rest of the Council regret the way they'd treated him *then*?

CHAPTER FIVE

Edvard was summoned to the bridge a moment after helping Jake, Ria and Tom in the passageway. His sister had called and wanted to speak to him urgently. Tom saw Ria and Jake to their room and left them, promising to meet them at breakfast as planned, only a little later than originally discussed.

Jake walked into their cabin and made straight for the plush couch, collapsing onto it while he caught his breath. His head was still whirling with everything he'd seen. Some visions were like that—time compressed into blurred images scrolling by in rapid succession.

It was hard to follow, but he'd had a lot of experience in sorting out the images. He began to make sense of what he'd seen as Ria moved around the room. She came to him, holding a glass of ice water in her hands. He might've sought something stronger but it was too early to be hitting the hard stuff—no matter how confusing the day had been already.

"Do you always have these visions so close together?" Ria spoke gently as she sat at his side on the couch. She put her arm around his shoulders, her hand pressing into his back, offering the comfort of touch that shifters found so appealing. Come to think of it, Jake found it appealing as well. Especially if it was Ria's touch.

"No, this was an anomaly. I think a lot of sh—" He stopped himself from cussing, though he'd already said a few things he probably shouldn't have in front of her. "Stuff," he corrected himself. "A lot of stuff is going down right now that I might be able to influence. It usually works like that. Most of the time, I see things pertaining to something or someone I know or can find. It seems to be tailored so that I can be useful, I guess. I've always found it handy, except when the stuff hits the fan, like it is right now."

"So the vision in your sleep was so you could help my Guard and your friend. And then this one was so you could warn the sea-based shifters." She seemed to be dealing with his quirks better than he'd hoped.

"I'm sorry you had to see me like that. I'd meant to give you a heads up before a big one hit, but I didn't have time. Usually I don't get like that often. Maybe once a year or so. I was going to warn you so you wouldn't be concerned when, or if, it happened and you were with me." Jake had been doing a lot of apologizing this morning and dawn had only just broken through their stateroom window.

Ria moved right into his lap and stroked his chin, which was covered in stubble, he realized belatedly. She didn't seem to mind, thank goodness. Her touch felt too good to lose.

"It's okay, Jake. There's a lot we need to discover about each other. I'm just glad Ed knew what was going on. I think you shocked poor Tom though." She chuckled and he began to see the humor in her words.

"Yeah, I bet he's never seen a guy zone out like that before," he agreed.

"No Jake…" she pulled back to look at him, meeting his gaze. "Your eyes… They swirled with power. It was like nothing I've ever seen and it was very clear you have deeply hidden depths of magic. I think Tom was both scared shitless, and impressed." She moved in to place a peck on his cheek. "By the way, you can say the word shit in front of me. I won't faint."

He pulled her closer, resting his forehead against hers.

"No, sweetheart. Give me an inch and I'll take a mile, just like any other guy. You're a lady. More than that, you're a queen. At least let me *try* to clean up my language around you. I can't promise I'll always remember to censor myself, but it's a small thing I can do to show you how much I respect you. And if we ever have kids, I don't want them picking up my bad habits."

Her breath caught when he mentioned them having children and he could see the longing in her eyes. He hadn't thought much about spawning before, but having Ria in his life was making him think about a lot of things he never really had before. He wanted it all with her. Kids. House in the 'burbs. White picket fence. Big backyard so she could run around in her furry form. Trees for the kids to climb. The whole enchilada.

He kissed her because he couldn't help himself. She was in his arms, warm, inviting and *his*. That was the kicker. She was his. She told him so in many subtle ways that made his heart skip a beat with wonder.

And he was hers. He would prove that to her over and over. As many times as it took for her to believe him. To believe *in* him. He might be human, but he would be the best mate he could to his little kitty.

She broke the kiss and moved back, giving his lips one last little lick with a flick of her tongue. Man, she turned him on. It wouldn't take much to be inside her. They were both wearing robes and he had nothing under his. But she was wrapped in a rubber band of a lycra bathing suit that wouldn't come off without a fight. Jake sighed as he set her aside and stood up.

"We both need a shower. Our skin doesn't thrive on salt water like the selkies." He took her hand, helping her to stand with exaggerated politeness before ushering her into the attached bath.

What followed was a quick, slippery session in the small shower where they both got rid of the salt on their skin while making each other crazy with wanting. What had started on the couch, moved to the shower and finished on the small vanity as Ria perched on the edge, accepting Jake's powerful thrusts.

As quickies went, it was spectacular. They were both breathless and feeling a lot mellower when he finally let her go. Jake supported her for a moment more because Ria's legs seemed kind of wobbly and he had to grin, knowing he'd made her weak in the knees. She had done the same to him, but he was a little better at hiding it.

She scooted back under the water in the shower for a quick rinse before joining him back in the cabin. He was already half-dressed when she came walking in, naked and beautiful. Jake stopped in his tracks, just watching her for a long moment. She noticed his fascination and smiled at him.

"You're going to have to get used to shifters being naked, Jake. We tend to strip a lot when we want to change shape. Or…" She walked closer, trailing her fingers up his arm while a teasing light filled her gorgeous eyes. "…when we want to play with our mates."

"I'm all for that," he answered, pulling her into his arms, his hands at her waist. Then he thought of something that had happened earlier. "But I'll have to object a bit when it seems you're enjoying the view a little too much."

She seemed to think for a moment then laughed. "Oh, you mean Tom? I won't deny, he's a good looking guy, but my mate is the only man I'm interested in making love to, now that I've found him." She reached up and tugged his head down for a quick kiss. "I'm never letting you go, Jake. I might appreciate the view from time to time—I'm a shifter, after all, and we're very sensual creatures, if you didn't realize that already—but I'll always belong wholly, completely and forevermore, to you." She kissed him again.

Before their kisses could escalate into something more, the phone in their cabin rang. Jake let her go and she scampered away to find clothing while he picked up the phone.

"Yeah, we'll be right out," he promised a laughing Tom on the other end of the line. Sure enough, the other shifter had figured they'd need a reminder to join the rest of the group for breakfast.

Jake reached for his shirt, watching Ria dress with economical movements. She was probably the only woman he had ever known who could get ready as quickly as he could. That was something he had to admire. She wasn't rushing, but she moved so gracefully—and quickly—and she looked like a million bucks no matter what. She was just beautiful, in every way.

Her compassion for her people and her kind heart were unexpected, but very welcome. Her unconscious regal bearing was tempered by sparkling humor and a down-to-earth quality that enchanted him. He looked forward to getting to know every last little thing about her, which was something he had never contemplated with any of his past girlfriends.

No, Ria was unique in every way and he looked forward to fulfilling that vision of them as an old, happy couple. If they lived that long.

Tom's sister turned out to be a young woman in her early twenties named Jacki. She was a Kinkaid, which is to say, a shifter. Ria figured on her for another selkie, though most of the large Kinkaid Clan were lions. A complicated mating centuries ago had produced a family line rich with magic and mixed heritage. Most were born lion-shifters but a few in every generation turned out to be selkies.

It seemed as if a large percentage of the Kinkaid selkies had concentrated around Sam's yacht. It made sense. Water was their element and the ocean their playground. Why not take a post on their Clan leader's yacht that would make everybody happy?

Jacki was friendly but reserved as she led them to the breakfast room. It was a huge dining room on yet another deck of the ship and it looked like a lot more people were joining them for the meal than Ria expected. By the looks of things, Edvard had called in the majority of the crew to hear what would be said. This had just gone from breakfast meeting to conclave in no time at all.

More people than Ria would have credited sat in the big room. There was a buffet set up along one side where platters of eggs, meats and all sorts of pastries and muffins were available. Many of the crew were availing themselves of the food, eating heartily while waiting for the meeting to begin.

The yacht had started moving while Ria and Jake were still in their cabin, which meant there was at least a small crew on the bridge and elsewhere actually running the boat while everyone else appeared to be gathered in the breakfast room. Edvard greeted them when they arrived and everyone fell silent, a hush of expectation filling the big room.

"Get some food while I start," Edvard instructed, indicating two seats next to him that had been left empty for them. Ria and Jake filled their plates at the buffet while Edvard went through duty rosters with the bulk of his crew and set the stage for what would come next.

Most of the others were eating or had empty plates in front of them, so Ria didn't feel awkward when she sat down beside Edvard and began to nibble on her breakfast. Her nerves were taut though, anticipating what would come next. Things were about to heat up again, if Jake's vision was anything to go by.

Edvard finished with ship business and turned to Jake and Ria, taking a moment to make introductions. "Most of you know we've been working with a human at Sam's request. Some of you know Jake from your military days." Edvard nodded toward a few of the men, Tom included. "What you probably didn't know is that he is a seer of great power." Surprised murmurs filled the room as Edvard went on. "Another thing you might not realize is that he was solely responsible for saving the *pantera noir* Nyx the other night. Milady, I think we've come to the point where my people need to know exactly who they are protecting."

Ria didn't like being put on the spot, but she understood. She usually did her best to fly under the radar with other shifters, preferring that they not know who she was. Her position brought with it a sacred duty that made many other shifters either uncomfortable with her, or clingy. She didn't like either response.

"It's okay," she told Edvard. "I don't know how far out we are. Will we be in port before tomorrow?"

"No, milady. Which is why I thought perhaps with the new moon peaking tomorrow..." Edvard trailed off, but she knew what he was driving at.

"I will be pleased to deliver messages to any of your people that seek them tonight, Captain." She knew her duty and saw the mix of hopeful and skeptical looks from those gathered in the room.

"Thank you," Edvard said formally, bowing his head slightly. "Now, as to the rest." He turned back to his people to speak to the crowd. "As I said, Jake is a seer, like my sister. Tom and I witnessed a vision overtake Jake earlier in the companionway, which was seconded by a call from my sister moments later. The *Venifucus* are on the move. They will awaken something this night that has not seen the light of day in centuries. From today forward, no one is to venture into the deeps. Even the shallows may not be safe. The ocean will be off limits to all for the next few months at least."

The murmurs turned to outright talking as the selkies and lions all around grew alarmed. "What did they see?" one person toward the front asked, looking from Edvard to Jake.

Edvard raised one eyebrow at Jake, ceding the floor to him.

"Some kind of evil creature of the deep," Jake replied. "They're going to free it tonight and there's no way to stop it. Anyone who tries, will die needlessly."

"It is the leviathan," Edvard intoned and several of the shifters gasped. "My sister recognized it. A thing of legend out of the ancient past. An immortal thing that has been locked up for centuries, to be freed by the evil servants of Elspeth." Edvard paused for a long moment, during which nobody moved. "But Jake's vision gives hope. This scourge will not foul our oceans forever." He turned to Jake, wordlessly asking him to reassure his people—many of whom were exceptionally tied to the ocean.

"There are two warriors who are of the water, but not of your race. They'll subdue the creature, if anyone can. They won't be called upon for several months, but at some point, they will do battle with the leviathan, and have a very good chance of winning. Nobody else has the skills and magic necessary to do the job, so it's best to not even try," Jake added as a warning.

"My sister concurs with every last word of what Jake has said, so I don't want any of you hatching plans to combat the leviathan. It is a job for those two warriors who will present themselves when the time is right." Edvard gave each one of the warriors in the room a stern look. "I also spoke to Sam a few minutes ago, and you are all to consider this an edict from the king and leader of our Clan. Stay out of the water. Don't go poking at the leviathan. Is that clear?"

Grudging murmurs of assent came from all around the room.

"Good. Now..." Edvard sat back in his chair. "Sam wants us to support the Nyx in whatever capacity we can. She is separated from her Royal Guard with only Jake—able as he is—as her protector. They are also newly mated." Smiles greeted this pronouncement. "We have one more night aboard before all hell breaks loose in our ocean. I suggest we make the most of it. Milady," he spoke to Ria, sitting at his side. "I know I sprang this on you. Do you have a preferred way of handling the new moon ceremony?"

Put on the spot, Ria cleared her throat. "I've never done it at sea before, but I guess we'll muddle through." She smiled, glad when one or two of the assembled shifters smiled back. "Can we do it on deck? Outdoors is best, under the dark moon."

"We'll prepare the sun deck. Tonight it'll be a moon deck," Edvard joked.

Jake spent the day with Edvard and the rest of his team,

making plans and describing in detail what he had seen. They were able to conference Edvard's sister into the conversation at one point, comparing visions and fleshing out parts of the scene that helped in the planning. Jake liked working with the woman, even though he'd never met her before. They understood each other when the rest of those listening in couldn't help.

He tried to keep tabs on what Ria was up to, but Edvard kept assuring him that she was all right. According to him, she was making preparations for the new moon ceremony—whatever that was. Jake had an inkling, of course. He knew—in principle—what the Nyx did on the nights surrounding the new moon. He just didn't know what sort of preparation was necessary or exactly how the event would unfold.

Edvard and the rather surprising squad of ex-Navy SEALs who were also selkies, kept Jake busy all day. They made plans and contingency plans. Jake was gratified to find that he wasn't on his own in protecting Ria. The selkies and lion shifters that made up the crew were volunteering to help him make sure she made it back to her Guard safely. And from the way they were talking, they would be around for some time after as well.

Jake was relieved. He knew that things were coming to a head for Ria and him. The future wasn't always crystal clear in his visions, but he knew they were going to need help sooner rather than later. He figured it would be up to him to call in a few old favors from his former comrades-in-arms, but this was even better.

These shifters knew the true value of what and who they were protecting. Kinkaid's people were all familiar with shifter monarchy and the importance of protecting their leaders. Many shifter communities around the world had suffered losses in the recent battles and they were doubly dedicated to preventing more death and disorder among their numbers. They were united in defiance of the *Venifucus* threat. The variations between species and Clans didn't make such a big difference anymore—not since the ancient evil had begun to rear its ugly head again.

By mid-afternoon, they had created a plan—and multiple contingency plans, should Plan A not work out as hoped—to regroup with Ria's Royal Guard in a mountainous region of North Carolina. They would dock the yacht as close as possible, then take an overland route to the area they had chosen. As it turned out, the spot they had decided on was the home territory of a group of werefoxes.

Ben and Ria's people had scouted out the Alpha of the group when they had arrived in the area, seeking his permission to stay and aid for their wounded. They hadn't meant to step on any toes, but it was hard to move in a sparsely populated mountainous area without running into one group of shifters or another. Pretty much wherever they ended up in the mountains, they would have to deal with the locals.

Foxes were cunning, but not quite as combative as say…lion shifters. Foxes knew when to cut and run. They also knew when to take a stand. Edvard had appealed directly to the Fox Alpha by phone earlier in the day, giving him a warning about what was coming in his direction, and a promise of alliance with the Kinkaid Clan if the foxes decided to help. Such a thing was not to be turned down lightly. The Kinkaids had immense power and wealth. Lions weren't called the king of the jungle for nothing. And the fact that Kinkaids had not only lions, but a significant number of extra-magical seal shifters under their banner made them a force to be reckoned with.

The Fox Alpha—a man named Georgio, who had young children to look out for—wisely decided to evacuate the non-combatants from the area. They, like most shifters, had a pre-arranged bolt-hole ready to go. It was a place they could evac to where the weaker members of their Clan could hide out under the protection of the warriors.

A squad of the fox Clan's best warrior-scouts would remain, to aid in any action that might arise. After all, they knew their territory better than anyone. Foxes, though not numerous, were strong allies of the Lords and all those who served the Light, the Alpha promised, and his people would live up to their alliances.

Jake was satisfied with the plan. He knew the showdown was going to happen in the woods. There was no more avoiding it. The situation had to come to a head and he knew it was better to guide events to a time and place where he could prepare to defend Ria as well as possible. They had allies he hadn't even contemplated before today, and a good shot at defeating the evil that was coming for his mate.

Mate. Now that was a new concept, but one he happily embraced. He had loved Ria from afar for far too long. Being with her was like every good dream he'd ever had, coming true all at once. He hadn't been able to express himself to her very well up 'til now. He was still coming to terms with the somewhat overwhelming enormity of what being with her in reality—instead of just in his visions—was really like.

He'd had to keep himself from daydreaming several times during the planning session. The other men didn't seem to mind, though he thought he intercepted a few pointed looks and veiled amusement from some of the older guys.

He couldn't have asked for a better group to help him defend his mate. Each and every one of these guys was a battle-hardened warrior. Most had multiple tours as combat-zone Special Operators. And they were all shifters. They had the cunning and instinct of their animal side combined with the intellect and experience of the human. It was a deadly combination. Deadly for their enemies, Jake prayed.

Ria was in true danger here and he wasn't able to see the outcome of the coming confrontation. His gift worked like that sometimes. It showed him the lead-up, and sometimes several different possible outcomes, but very often, it didn't show him the outcome of a single, key event that was crucial to the possible futures. It was a hinge point. A nexus.

Tomorrow would decide not only Ria and his fate, but the fate of millions of shifters all over the world. He only hoped he'd been convincing enough to the allied warriors gathered all around. He thought they understood the importance of what they were going to do in those mountains, but he was never really able to express the true depth of his visions in plain language. It was something you had to see and feel to really understand. Words just couldn't capture the true nature of his vision.

As they wrapped up the meeting, Edvard slapped Jake on the back and steered him toward a deck he hadn't yet explored. He had wanted to go back to the cabin to see if Ria was there and to freshen up a bit, but Edvard wasn't letting him get away that easily.

When he cleared the last stair and saw what waited up on one of the observation decks, he understood why Ed was so insistent. The crew had set up a party. A buffet groaned under the weight of platters of food. Decorations had been found somewhere and put up. Colorful streamers gave the deck a festive air. And Ria was already there, standing by the bar, surrounded by women.

But the crowd was quiet, watching him with eager smiles on their faces. They parted to let him through as he walked directly to Ria. He stopped in front of her, aware of the curious onlookers only in a peripheral way. Ria was all he saw, really. Her smile filled his world.

Jake went to one knee before her, taking her hand in his. By that simple gesture, he declared his loyalty, his allegiance, and his love. There was no need for words. Ria's eyes filled with tears, but they were happy ones. She reached down to kiss him and he stood, taking her into his arms and returning the kiss with all the depth of emotion pent up inside him.

Wolf whistles finally penetrated his hearing as the shifters all around them whooped and applauded. This was a party and the shifters were ready to celebrate.

Jake pulled back, looking down into Ria's upturned face. "The party is for us?" he asked, just to be certain.

"Yeah. An impromptu mating celebration, since they knew we wouldn't have a chance to celebrate with my Clan for some time yet." Unspoken between them was the added *if ever.*

Everyone knew they were up against something grave here and might not make it out alive. This party then, was to celebrate a mating while they still could. Tomorrow might never come, but today, by the Goddess, they would party.

CHAPTER SIX

The spur of the moment party touched Ria deeply. Her life had seldom included such commonplace things as a simple mating party. Most shifters loved to party, but Ria had lived most of her life on the run, never being able to settle in one place for too long. The nature of the duties she had assumed when she took over as Nyx from her mother demanded that she give up a normal life. She was at the mercy of what she was. Who she was, underneath it all, didn't really seem to matter…except maybe to Jake.

Since meeting him, she finally understood what mating was all about. Having just one person in the entire world who was devoted to *you*, and you alone. It was a heady feeling. And even though she had the occasional doubt about his ability to form a true mate bond because he was human, most of the time she thought they were both on the same page. Both devoted and loyal.

It didn't matter to him that she was a queen of her people. It didn't matter to her that he was a seer. All that mattered when they were together was each other. As it should be between mates.

"Normally, this kind of party would go on all night long, you know," she told her mate as they danced to a slow tune someone had put on.

There were speakers placed discretely around the deck, and a superior sound system. They had music, the fresh air of the early evening breeze, good food and even better company. Who could ask for more from a celebration of their mated happiness?

"I'll count on an all-nighter when we finally get to have our mating celebration among your Clan," he replied, nuzzling her neck. She loved it when he did that, but he drew back, his eyes narrowed in question. "But I suspect you have other plans for this evening—or at least part of it."

"Yeah. About that." She sighed, knowing she couldn't put off her explanation any longer. "You know about what I do, right? I mean, you've seen something in your visions that shows you the gift and burden of being the Nyx, haven't you?"

"You speak for those on the other side of the veil," he answered in all seriousness, his voice a low tone that only she could hear. She answered in kind, though the shifters around them were giving them as much privacy as they could on the wide deck. The soft whisper of the evening breeze was enough to keep her words from falling on ears other than her mate's.

"I do. There's a ceremony centered around it all, but at the heart of the thing is the object everyone is after." She didn't want to name it. It was second-nature to her to obscure the fact of the amulet's existence. It was the greatest secret of the Nyx. "I use it to communicate with the other side, but only on the days surrounding the new moon, for a few hours each night for three nights. During that time, any shifter is entitled to try to speak with those who have passed beyond our realm. It's my duty to try to intercede for any who asks."

"This time, Ria..." he pulled back to look down into her eyes. His expression was solemn. "This time, you had better start seeking some answers yourself. Time is running out. You need to know if there's anything those on the other side can tell you that will help in your defense. Don't ignore them again. Talk to them first, this time. Promise me."

She took a deep breath and let it out, finally having to face her fears. "Okay. But I want you nearby. I've been afraid to listen to what they had to say. I was afraid they were warning me that I was going to be joining them soon. I didn't see how I could keep running the way I was for much longer. I thought my time was up on this mortal plane."

"Nope." His expression softened as he drew her closer, still softly swaying to the music. "Everything's different now. I'm with you. We are one. Where you go, I go, forevermore."

"You almost sound like a shifter," she teased him. "Have you been studying up?"

"Actually, yeah. For a very long time." His tone grew serious. "There's a lot you don't know about me and my past. A lot of it you'll find out along the way and I look forward to discovering each new facet of you over time, but one thing you need to understand right now is that I can protect you. I've trained as hard as any of your Guard. And I've sought teaching from places your Guard would never think to go. I wasn't kidding about meeting Sam at the snowcat enclave. I spent a lot of time in Tibet, working with the mystics there— both shifter and human. The human monks helped with my gift. The snowcats taught me…well…a lot of other useful things. Things that have prepared me for this task. For our lives together, Ria." He was so serious, she nearly stopped moving, but he made sure to talk so quietly that it felt like they were alone in the crowd and only she could hear him.

"You've spent a lot of time preparing, it sounds like," she commented.

"Preparing for this, Ria. For you. For us," he agreed. "When push comes to shove—and it will sooner than we want—you need to know you can count on me. Don't count me out just because I'm human. You've only seen a small portion of what I can do."

She smiled as he did. That last bit could be taken many ways and she chose to lighten the mood. They had been serious too long. This was a party, after all.

"Sounds intriguing." She gave him a mischievous smile

and batted her eyes. He allowed the change in the tenor of their conversation as the music picked up and they parted.

Edvard claimed her as dance partner while Jake ended up dancing with Jacki Kinkaid. Everyone looked like they were having a good time and laughter abounded. This was one of the nicest surprises anyone had ever given her and Ria would treasure it—and these generous people—always.

A few hours later, when the dark moon was making its trek toward zenith, Jake sat near Ria on a small deck near the very top of the massive ship, watching her make her preparations for the ceremony during which she would commune with the other side. She had pulled him aside about fifteen minutes before, drawing him away from the party, which was still going on somewhere below them, though from the sound of it, things were beginning to wind down as the night deepened.

"It won't be long now," Ria said, straightening the cloth in front of her. "I can feel the moon shifting into position."

Ria was sitting under the dark of the moon, on the deck, her legs folded gracefully under her in an almost meditative position. To her right was a chilled bottle of water. To her left was a snowy white cloth napkin. In front of her was an ornamental bowl with water in it that reflected the moonlight.

Since the yacht was underway, the bowl wasn't exactly full. The water sloshed a little when they encountered a rough patch of ocean, but the sea was mostly calm, thankfully.

"I don't really need any of this," Ria said softly, so that only Jake could hear. "It's all for show, really, but having some kind of ceremony seems to comfort people. It makes it more special for them, I think." She uncapped the bottle of water and took a sip before placing it back at her side. "They'll be arriving shortly."

"Remember sweetheart, you are going to seek your own answers first this time," he reminded her. He saw the fear in her eyes. Heard it in her nervous chatter.

"Yeah, I know. That's why I left a little early. I'll do it,

77

but…" She reached out to him, taking his hand in hers. "Just stay with me, okay."

"I'm with you." He replied in a steady, low voice. "I won't leave you."

She reached for the chain around her neck, pulling it from under her shirt. Hanging from the chain was a small, diamond-shaped pendant that gleamed dully in the darkness.

"This is what all the fuss is about. And you are the first human in centuries to even see this amulet. I wanted you to know, so you would understand what we are guarding. If this falls into the wrong hands, it's conceivable that it could be used to breach the veil between worlds, though I suppose it would probably burn out the amulet in the process. It wasn't designed to open physical gateways, merely to allow communication on occasion."

"I'm honored you would share the secret with me," Jake replied in as serious a tone as she had used. This was a big step for her, he realized.

"They're gathering," she whispered, her focus on something beyond him.

Jake looked over his shoulder, assuming she was talking about the shifters on the vessel, but there was no one on the deck or anywhere around that he could see. That's when he realized what she had meant. He turned back to her and watched as her eyes lost their focus completely and her head dropped forward for a long moment.

He wanted to check on her, but he also didn't want to disrupt anything that might be happening on the spiritual plane. That was as good a term as any that he could think of for the plane on which she was somehow communicating with those spirits who had passed to the other side.

He watched her for long, long moments, aware of the sounds of the party below fading into nothingness as the crowd dispersed. Jake had the sense that many of the shapeshifters who had helped them celebrate their mating were now waiting—just out of sight below this highest of the ship's decks—for some sign that they should approach. Jake wouldn't give that sign, or allow anyone to interfere, until Ria gave him the go-ahead. This time was for her. She needed to talk to those who waited beyond the veil to speak with her.

For too long, she had ignored those who had come to deliver warnings and impart knowledge. Now was her time to use the hereditary power of the Nyx to learn how to save the world from truly terrible evil.

Jake watched over her silent communication. Her eyes took on a ghostly light that made them glow slightly in the dark night. The stars shone down brightly, though the moon kept a dark vigil over them all.

After more than a half hour, Ria nodded and came back to herself, her gaze seeking Jake's. He could see that she was still distracted by whatever she saw or heard on the other plane, but she also saw him. He knew it from the slight smile on her lips as she met his gaze.

"I understand," she whispered, looking at him, but clearly talking to someone else. Then her vision cleared a little more, the glow fading slightly from her eyes as she saw him fully. "I'm ready for the others now. Let them come up. There are many on the other side who wish to speak."

Her eyes went hazy again as Jake lifted one hand, signaling those who had gathered by the stairs to come up. Silently, the shifters moved closer, forming a semi-circle around Ria and Jake, each taking a seat on the floor of the deck, watching her intently. Jake rearranged himself to sit at Ria's side, slightly forward. He would be able to leap between her and any physical attack, though he sensed no ill intent coming from the gathered shifters. On the contrary, there was a feeling of excitement and anticipation in the air.

Ria seemed aware of the people gathered on the deck, though she kept her gaze lowered to the bowl of water in front of her. She dipped her fingers into the bowl, swirling the water for a moment, then allowing it to still. She spoke some words that were mere whispers Jake couldn't make out.

The water in the bowl stilled and a bit of fog rose from the bowl. Jake hadn't seen how she managed it. It could have been magic or perhaps some kind of illusion, but the shifters certainly believed the bowl had a lot to do with Ria's abilities. By design, he supposed. Nobody really knew how the Nyx's power worked...except Ria, and now Jake. And maybe somehow the *Venifucus*, which didn't bear thinking about at the moment.

"And so it begins," Ria said softly, raising her glowing gaze to the gathering. There were murmurs toward the back of the deck and a few audibly gasped at her altered appearance. It was clear that something special was happening here.

"Kinkaids," Ria said in a strong voice. "The African Leo is here and wishes it to be known that although he was skeptical at first, he is pleased by the new blood leading his people. Tell Sam that he has his predecessor's blessing, though he knows it will be an uphill battle to unite some of the African Clans under a white lion's rule." She went on to describe particular bits of advice the former leader of all lion shifters had for the new one. Since Sam Kinkaid wasn't here, the information was dutifully taken down by his kinsmen and would be passed on.

"Josiah," Ria said after the lion leader had finished his message. A handsome young warrior, standing toward the back, near Edvard, raised his hand uncertainly. Ria's glowing eyes rested on him. "Your grandmother wishes me to say how proud she is of you and that she is sorry to have left you so soon. You are right. She was murdered. She did not accidentally drown as the reports claimed. She was tackled from behind and hit on the head with a rock, then held down until she drowned. You will have a chance for vengeance shortly and she wants you to be careful. The one who killed her wears the *Venifucus* tattoo on her hand. You cannot see it, but there is a woman who will fight at your side. She has the ability to see such things. Trust her when she tells you who is marked and who is not. Even if it seems wrong, she sees the truth."

Jake watched the man's reaction and saw the surprise when he was first called by name, followed by anger and determination once Ria delivered her message. He seemed to understand exactly what Ria was saying about his grandmother and he looked ready to charge into battle to avenge the old lady.

Jake was impressed with the detail of Ria's messages. He had half expected the messages to be of the vague variety often given by so-called psychic mediums on popular television shows, but this was something else altogether. The details were specific and the messages clear.

She gave simple messages of love from lost family and friends. Messages of warning and of importance about things those on the other side had left undone. Blessings for marriages and new children. All sorts of things that were incredibly specific and undeniably touching for those who had the rare chance to hear from lost loved ones.

It was reassuring in a way, especially for Jake. He was human. Beliefs about an afterlife varied greatly from culture to culture and Jake was reassured to hear that the next realm was something undeniably real. He had adopted a mostly shifter attitude toward religion, life, and death early on in his studies, but even he had doubted the existence of other realms—especially the idea that the spirit went on, into another realm after it left this place.

Ria kept talking for a couple of hours or more. She drank from the water bottle at her side occasionally, but her eyes kept their unearthly glow and her voice changed depending on the kind of message she delivered. Sometimes tender, sometimes tough, she seemed to strive to convey the actual tone she was receiving from those whose messages she delivered. She was the conduit—the means by which they could communicate with the mortal realm—and both sides seemed to respect that.

She often said *you're welcome* after delivering a message. It became clear she was accepting the thanks of the spirit for having relayed the message as well as those of the person in the mortal realm who had received it.

She kept going, but Jake could see the toll it took on her.

She seemed to give of her own energy to keep the connection strong, losing a bit of her sparkle as the session wore on. He kept one eye on his watch, wondering how much more of this she could take until finally, she called a halt.

"This is the final message before the window closes for another cycle of the moon. The departed wish you all to know that we face great danger and we must face it alone. They cannot help us in what will come and even they do not know how it will all turn out. The message is one of perseverance. The message is a reminder of our duty to the Goddess and to Her Light. A reminder of our pledge to serve good and fight evil. For what we are facing is the truest evil that has ever manifested in our mortal realm. It was defeated once and it has sought to return here ever since. It has not ever gotten this close to victory before and it is our task to keep it from triumphing." The glow started to fade from her eyes. "We must win," she whispered before the magic was gone entirely and she slumped, her head down, her arms at her sides.

The ritual was over and Jake could see that Ria was completely drained. The shifters got up silently and filed off the deck, heading back to their duties. Many looked back at Ria as if to say something or offer to help, but then they saw Jake there, at her side and some nodded, knowing he would look out for her.

Finally only Edvard was left. He came over and collected the bowl and other accoutrements Ria had used while Jake lifted her into his arms. She was completely drained and didn't object as he carried her down to their cabin. Edvard took care of the cleanup while Jake took care of his lady.

Ria slept for a few hours, waking in the middle of the night to find herself wrapped in Jake's strong arms. She didn't really remember how she had gotten from the upper deck where the ritual had been held to her cabin, but she knew Jake had orchestrated it. She hadn't been left so drained by a new moon ritual in a long time, but she had felt it important to push herself this time—to give as many messages as she could, in case she never got a chance to do so again.

She was a realist. Her chances of survival during the coming struggle weren't good. She had been dodging one threat or another most of her life but all the things she had learned from the ancestors during those first few minutes of contact last night had her worried. Truly worried.

She snuggled into Jake's arms, glad he was with her. She had never known such happiness as when she was with him. If she did fail and ended up joining the ancestors on the other side of the veil, at least she had known this short time with Jake—her true mate. She had never really thought she would find a man as amazing as him. A mate of her heart that her inner cat not only respected but loved as much as her human heart did. Jake was it for her. The perfect man to share her life with—if she had a life after the danger that was coming.

He had saved her ass once already, and in a very dramatic fashion with that helicopter rescue, but could they keep preventing disaster again and again? The enemy wouldn't give up easily. Somehow, one of the *Venifucus* leaders knew her secret. The ancestors had been very specific about that. Only one knew of the amulet.

"I can feel you tensing up." Jake's voice came to her out of the darkness of the cabin and she realized she must have awoken him with her worries. His arms tightened around her and she was grateful for his warm presence.

"I spoke to my mother." She tried not to let emotion affect her, but she couldn't help the way her voice cracked on her whispered admission.

"Oh, sweetheart," Jake turned her in his arms, and hugged her tight, kissing her temple, her cheek, her ear and moving down to her neck, offering comfort. "I'm sorry."

"It's okay," she was quick to reassure him. "She's never come forward before and she died a long time ago. She was Nyx before me. It passes down through the maternal line and she was away on business when she was attacked and killed. She had left the amulet among her belongings and I knew where it was and what it did. She had raised me with the knowledge, though not even our Guards knew the real secret behind her power."

"When did she die?" Jake asked. It was about time he figured a few things out. Ria knew she looked a lot younger than she really was and she fostered that illusion.

"About ten years ago," she admitted. "When I was seventeen."

"Wait a minute." Jake leaned up on one elbow, looking down at her in the dim light. "You're twenty-seven?"

He seemed more amused than upset so she smiled. "Yeah. Shifters live a long time and age a bit differently than humans. Plus, I've fostered the young image so people would underestimate me. How's it feel to be my boy toy?"

He laughed and she was reassured by his reaction. "You're not that much older than me, sweetheart. But you definitely pulled one over on me this time. I thought you were in your late teens or early twenties—older than you look, but not by much."

"Disappointed?" She looked at him carefully gauging his reactions.

"How can you even ask that?" He tucked his arm around her and drew her close so he could kiss her. "You're my perfect mate, Ria, no matter how old you are."

"Glad to hear it because I feel the same way about you," she admitted, kissing him deeply as he made her forget the scary things she'd learned for a little bit.

He let her go and a devilish sort of smile lit his face as he looked at her.

"What?" She just knew he was up to something.

"I was just thinking. If I'm your boy toy, then you should be my sex kitten. What do ya say? Fair's fair, and all that, right?"

She pretended to consider his playful words. "What exactly are a sex kitten's duties?"

"Let's see." He rubbed his hands over her body as he thought about it. They were both naked, which was a good start, she thought. "I think you have to try to seduce me a lot. Not that I'll be all that hard to seduce, but I might make you work for it occasionally."

She grabbed his butt playfully. "You'll make me work for it, huh? How exactly do you expect to manage that?" She lifted her leg, her thigh rubbing against the part of him that was already getting hard.

"With you? Not easily, that's for sure." He chuckled as he dipped his head to nibble on her neck. "But a man has his pride."

She reached down between them and wrapped her hand around his hardness, holding his gaze. "Yeah, I'd say you've got quite a bit to be proud of here."

He laughed, even as his breath caught. "I don't think you need any help with the sex kitten thing, Ria. You've got the part down pat."

She reached forward, licking his jaw with a quick motion before kissing her way to his lips. After that, things moved fast and there wasn't a lot of talking. He rolled her over and the covers fell to the floor as they hastily came together.

He thrust inside her even as she grabbed his ass to encourage him. Her inner cat was purring against his chest, which seemed to excite him even more. Good. That was good. He wasn't turned off by the evidence of her inner beast.

They faced each other, breathing hard as he did all the work this time. She was still a little drained from the ceremony, but she was swiftly gaining strength as her mate saw to her most basic needs. The desire and passion she felt in his arms was invigorating. The way he made love to her gave her hope for the future and a desire to remain in the present—in his embrace—for as long as they could manage.

But her body had other ideas. Her insides clamped down on him as a small climax hit her unexpectedly. Jake looked into her eyes as she came, holding his own climax back, watching her, making the moment even more intimate. And then he flipped her over.

Dragging her ass back toward him as he knelt behind her, he gave her what the cat craved. The world might call this position doggy-style, but it worked really well for cats too. The panther screeched in her mind, loving the dominant possession of its mate. The cat made no distinction between Jake and the fact that he couldn't turn furry. It was simply devoted to him—in any form. As was the woman.

His thrusts increased, pushing her to another climax, this one much higher than the previous. She strained against him, pushing backward to meet his thrusting hips, grinding against him as his hands guided her hips with strong, sure motions. Then all coherent thought fled as the pace increased once more into a frenzy of climax and completion the likes of which she had never felt before.

Her mate. Jake, the incredible man, had given her exactly what she needed, and he took care of her even as their shared orgasm peaked, then faded slowly, depositing them back to earth with a feather light caress, landing them both back on the soft bed.

Jake took care of her, repositioning her nearly boneless body next to him, his arm wrapped around her even as they both faded into sleep. She had never felt safer or more protected than she did in her mate's arms.

CHAPTER SEVEN

They made it to port later the next afternoon. Jake and Ria had slept in a little, though they were both up on the bridge with Edvard when they made port. Plans were made and adjusted as necessary. Travel was arranged and diversions coordinated. Edvard was using every one of his crew members to help hide the Nyx's tracks.

He was also pulling every Kinkaid Clan member off the ocean and waterways and had already sent out warnings to the *were* Lords and other shifter monarchs all around the world. Water-born creatures on the side of Light had to be warned. The Leviathan would rise tonight, according to the seers.

Jake was glad they were taking his warning seriously. A few times in the past he'd had trouble getting people to listen to him. Not in recent years, but it had happened often enough when he was younger to make him worry that some still wouldn't listen.

"Transport is coming for everyone," Edvard said as he got off the phone and turned to Jake. "I'll be along as soon as I secure the ship. We're going to ward it as best we can, but I want you two to take the helicopter, as discussed. I've got teams in place, ready to meet you in the mountains."

Ria stepped forward. "I can never thank you or Sam

enough for helping us, Edvard," she said formally. "I'm sorry to have brought danger to your vessel."

"I'm glad you both were here to warn us, lass," Edvard corrected her. "I hate to think what would have happened to my people without Jake's foresight." Edvard reached over to shake Jake's hand and then turned to give Ria a hug.

"Your sister would have seen it," Jake said, knowing that either way, the selkies would have had warning. He was just glad he had been there to work with Sophia by phone so they could fill in details each had missed. Together they had arrived at a much clearer vision than either would have had alone. "Please thank her again for working with me," Jake added.

One day, he hoped to meet the reclusive seer and compare notes. There was so much he still really didn't know about his gift. Any opportunity to talk with another who suffered from the same affliction was rare and worth pursuing.

"If all goes well over the next few days, you will have a chance to thank her in person soon," Edvard said with a smile. "I spoke to her last night. She wanted me to thank *you*," he emphasized the turnabout. "She was very impressed by the clarity of your vision and thought you worked well together. Our people are glad you were both available to consult with each other. I think you have both saved many lives this day—and you haven't even begun the real task yet." Edvard's continued grin said he was looking forward to the battle.

Jake wished he could be as gung ho. In seasons past he would have been, but now, everything had changed. He had Ria to worry about now. Her safety preyed on his mind. He'd only just found her. He couldn't lose her now.

Edvard looked from Jake to Ria and back again and Jake thought the older man understood his concerns. Edvard nodded once more and turned to look out over what he could see of the large ship from the wall-to-wall windows on the bridge.

"We're almost done here. My people have secured the

docks and the helicopter is ready. Now would be a good time to make your exit. We will keep anyone on the ground busy, but I suspect you have ideas about how to vary your flight plan to stay out of danger as much as possible, no?"

"Yessir," Jake answered, realizing it was time to go. Much as he wanted to hide out on this floating luxury resort and pretend they were safe, he knew better. "We'll be going directly. See you on the other side."

"If not before," Edvard agreed with a determined expression. "Good hunting, my friends, and may the Lady's Light shine on you."

"Good hunting, Uncle Ed." Ria gave him one last, impulsive hug and then turned away. Jake followed her off the bridge and they headed quickly toward the helipad.

The supplies and weapons Edvard had provided were already in the chopper. Jake had checked and rechecked everything already. He did a quick status check once more before he fired up the engine and took off as quickly as possible. He had one chance to make a clean getaway. Edvard's people were securing the area in and around the port. It would be up to Jake to pick a safe flight path that would take them where they needed to go.

They flew fast and as covertly as they could. Ria was impressed with Jake's flying abilities once again as he maneuvered the helicopter in unexpected ways over the least congested airspace he could find. He was taking an oblique approach to the area they wanted.

He had explained that there might possibly be forces on the ground that could try to shoot them down—if they could find them. Which was why he was flying high and fast...and on a rather creative route.

They had to fly over a large swath of the state to get to the mountains. They were aiming for a small sector in the Great Smoky Mountains National Park. A secretive little mountain ridge where everyone was a shifter and the dominant group was a Pack of fox families.

"Mount Sterling isn't far now," Jake reported via the headsets they had both donned in order to hear each other speak over the noise of the chopper blades. "There's a pretty famous lookout at the peak, but we're aiming for a more secluded section of the ridge about four miles from the peak." He executed a few maneuvers that she assumed were for their protection. "There's a cabin and a group of hidden caverns where the shifter families live. There's also a circle of stones at the highpoint of the ridge but the whole area is protected magically and by some pretty interesting topography that keeps the humans away, for the most part. We're going to land in a small clearing..." he trailed off as he dropped altitude.

Ria saw the ridge of a mountain in front of them and it looked like the spine of some great animal. As they drew closer, she felt the energy of the place and realized there was a huge concentration of magic nearby. This was a special place, indeed.

"There it is," Jake said, bringing in the chopper on a rapid approach.

Ria held her breath while he expertly piloted the helicopter into an impossibly small clearing. It was little more than a tiny hole in the otherwise dense forest along one side of the ridge on a mostly flat outcropping. But his skills were up to the test and he brought them to a gentle stop. One minute they were above the trees, the next they were surrounded by thick pine forest on all sides, with the rotors spinning down.

"There's Ben," Jake said as he took off his headset. She followed his line of sight to a tall man walking slowly out of the tree line. He was making some odd gestures with his hands and she saw Jake breathe easier. "Perimeter is secure. Everything is safe for now. It's okay to get out."

Jake threw open his door and quickly came around to her side to help her down. She grabbed the satchel of goodies Edvard had given her—a change of clothes and some other items—and joined him on the ground. After that harrowing ride, she was glad to have solid earth under her feet once again.

She realized they weren't on dirt. No, this area was clear because it was scraped down to the rock from which the mountains had formed. No topsoil meant nothing could grow in this little patch. Handy.

"Ria, this is Ben Steel," Jake made the introductions. Ria held out her hand to the other man and was pleased by the way he met her gaze. He might be human, but he was a strong example of his species.

"Thank you for helping my people," she said, wanting to be sure to get that out of the way first. More than anything, she wanted to see her Guard, but she also didn't want to disrespect this human's effort on their behalf. "Are they nearby?" Ria was a little puzzled that at least one of her Guard hadn't come out to meet her.

"They're on perimeter watch. As soon as you get into the trees, they'll come out. We want to be cautious of any satellite surveillance the enemy might have access to. In fact..." Ben took the baseball cap off his own head and plunked it down on Ria's with little ceremony. "Let's get you under cover of the canopy, ma'am."

"Good idea," Jake added as they made a dash for the trees which weren't all that far away. Ben stopped as she handed his hat back to him.

"I'll secure the chopper and do what I can for camouflage," he said to Jake as Ria felt rather than saw her Guard converge on a path toward her. Ben turned away as Jake thanked him and within seconds, they were surrounded.

Dorian reached her first, bowing his head slightly, though he never lowered his eyes, as was proper protocol among their people.

"My queen, it's good to see you in one piece," Dorian said with genuine warmth. His lips twitched up into a smile she felt herself responding to in kind.

"It's good to be in one piece, Dor. How's Bronson?"

"On my feet, milady," Bronson replied in a chipper voice as he bounded up beside her.

He was so young, so full of energy. The thought that he might've died just a few days ago was abhorrent to her. She reached out to take his hand, surprising him with a hug that he returned awkwardly.

"I'm sorry you got hurt, my friend, and I'm glad to see you on your feet again," she whispered before letting him go. She wasn't surprised to feel a couple of tears gathering in her eyes, but they didn't fall, for which she was grateful.

Shelly and Burgess came forward next, greeting her and assuring her all was well. They were the most seasoned of her current Guard and they more or less led the rest. They gave her an update on the situation as they escorted her through the trees, Jake trailing behind.

When they led her around to the back door of a cabin, she went in with them, aware of Jake following. The back entrance had tree cover while the front of the place had a slight clearing, which could probably be seen from a satellite. When they were all inside the small building, she turned to Jake and motioned him forward. He had a closed expression on his face, and she saw the resistance on the faces of her Guard, but this confrontation had to happen and now was better than later.

"Everyone, this is Jake, the man who swept me out of your presence the other night and brought me to safety. He is also my mate."

"Mate?" Shelly gasped, unable to hide her shock. The others seemed to handle their surprise and alarm a little better.

"Yeah, Shel, he's my true mate and a powerful seer. He knew where and when to be there to save me and he's foreseen things that may help us in our fight against the *Venifucus*. Give him a chance."

"I'm sorry, milady. It just took me by surprise. He's human? Or mage?" Shelly's confusion was clearly evident.

"Human, yes," Jake answered standing at Ria's side. "Mage, no. Just a seer. That's my one trick."

"And it's a helluva trick to have," Ben Steel said, coming

through the front door of the cabin and closing it behind himself. "Saved our asses more than once when we served together," he went on. "Don't you be doubting my boy Jake over there," he said to the *pantera* Guards. "He's as good as they come and he can probably best any one of you in hand-to-hand."

"Now that I'd like to see," Bronson muttered just a little too loud.

Ria bristled. "Instead of fighting among ourselves, shouldn't we all be preparing for what's to come from our enemy?" Jake's hand on her waist tried to soothe her, but she didn't like the way her people disrespected her mate. They would learn to respect him, or they would learn to be elsewhere. She didn't want anyone around her and Jake who didn't take her choices seriously. And who she chose to mate with was the most important choice she had ever made, as far as she was concerned.

Mating was for life. It was destiny. A shifter didn't really *choose* a mate. Their mate was chosen for them long before they were ever born. In all the world there was only one special soul that matched theirs and it was up to each shifter to find that perfect match. When that happened, it was a true mating, and anyone who doubted Ria's claims about Jake being her perfect mate didn't belong in their inner circle.

There wasn't time to fix that right now, when they were all facing a serious threat, but at the earliest opportunity, there would probably have to be a shakeup among her Royal Guard. Anyone who wouldn't accept Jake would have to find someplace else to work. Jake was the most important person in her life now and if her protectors couldn't accept that, then they weren't the friends she thought they had been.

"Don't worry, love. They'll come around in time," Jake whispered near her ear.

"Do we have that kind of time?" She looked up at him, turning her neck to the side to meet his gaze. His eyes grew troubled and she knew they didn't have the luxury of time without him even saying one word.

"Sitrep," she demanded, lowering her satchel to the table at the center of the large room. She sat and her people did likewise, except for Shelly, who kept watch by the back door.

Burgess delivered the report she'd demanded. "The foxes are watching the front. Ben's got a few friends in the area as well, which he'll tell you about in a minute," Burgess gestured toward the human who had taken a seat next to Jake. "We called for reinforcements and the beta team will arrive within the hour. They're coming by ground. The foxes have set up a watch on the single road below the ridge and will guide the beta team up here. I expect notification of their arrival at the base of the ridge any minute now." He looked at his cell phone, then placed it down on the table. "The fox Alpha wants a meeting, as per custom. He's a very understanding guy, and he's helped us—mostly because his mate is a seer and demanded he do so." Burgess nodded toward Jake with a touch of skepticism in his gaze that he couldn't quite hide, but Ria let it go for now. "She took the non-combatants and half his soldiers to safety. They've left half their soldiers— about a dozen—to act as guides and scouts for us. So far, they've lived up to their end of our bargain and I have no reason to doubt their sincerity."

"Why so trusting?" Ria asked, knowing Burgess was usually the most cautious of her people.

"There was also a priestess among their Pack and there's a stone circle not far from here. The priestess and the female Alpha together are quite a force to be reckoned with. They are half-sisters and it's clear they are on our side."

"Half-sisters?" Ria tried to puzzle that out.

"Yeah, their mother was human. She was married to a human first and the priestess was the result. He died out here in the woods on a camping trip. A fox male found the woman and her little girl and rescued them. They were mated not long after and their daughter subsequently mated the current Alpha once she had grown up." Burgess presented the facts, but Ria sensed there was much more to the story. He had to have had quite a conversation with the foxes to get into that kind of detail about their personal lives.

"All right," she said, accepting his judgment on the trustworthiness of the fox Pack for the moment. "So what are our numbers?"

"A dozen fox scouts. The four of us and the entire beta team—that's eight more—within the hour," Burgess replied quickly, then looked at Ben Steel.

"Me plus three other ex-commandos, who are working with the fox scouts at the moment, getting the lay of the land. I'll be sending one man up top to the stone circle to set up a guidance beacon that will help a few more friends drop in." Ben smiled as if he had a juicy secret and Ria couldn't wait to hear what the resourceful human had up his sleeve.

"Enough with the cat-who-swallowed-the-canary grin, already," Jake groused with a chuckle. "Who's coming?"

"A full platoon of Moore's men," Ben said with a broad grin. "I made a few calls and Burgess helped authorize the whole thing."

Burgess sat back, clearly pleased as he spread his hands on the table. "I called Cade and he was able to pull a few strings," he admitted. "You can't get better backup than the Wraiths."

Ria had heard of the secretive group that was mentioned only in whispers. That the humans knew about them was surprising. She looked at Jake with one eyebrow raised in question.

"Jesse Moore is a legend in Special Forces circles. Nobody knew he was a shifter except for people like me, and a chosen few. A lot of his fellow ex-Spec Ops shifter friends have congregated around him in Wyoming. It's known in certain circles that they hire out for worthy causes."

"Can't get much worthier than this," Burgess agreed. "The minute he knew who was asking for help, he agreed to send a full platoon. He would've sent more, he said, but they've been stretched pretty thin with all the action lately. He's not even charging their usual fee. Only asked for expenses so they could get here fast."

"Wow," Ria said, laughing a bit at her own lack of eloquence. She was surprised at the caliber of help they had been able to summon. Maybe they did stand a chance up here on this lonely mountain ridge after all.

Burgess's phone beeped and he flipped it over to check the screen. "They're here," he reported. "The scouts are bringing them up now. Should be at the cabin in about twenty minutes since they're coming in two-legged with supplies." Everyone knew the Guards—who were all shifters—could've gotten there faster on four feet, but without the gear that would come in handy when they were in their human forms.

"That ought to be enough time to meet with the local Alpha," Ria realized. "I think I've kept him waiting long enough." She stood and everyone else rose as well. Ria's Guard surrounded her as she made her way toward the back door.

"The Alpha's den is only a short distance away," Ben said, acting as guide.

She and Jake followed Ben, with two of her Guard as escort, toward what looked like a rock formation. Instead of just a pile of rocks, it was the cleverly concealed entrance to a cavern system that held all the conveniences of home. Rather than rudimentary cave dwellings, these cunning foxes had created a unique sort of home, hidden from view, beneath the spine of the ridge.

Ria had no idea how far back the caverns extended, but she was very impressed by both the quality of the furnishings and the ease of defense. There appeared to be only one way in or out and it was a narrow, hidden corridor with twists and turns that led through a high rock formation. Snipers could easily pick off anyone who tried to come in that way. Ria sensed though, that there were back entrances and connecting caves in this underground maze that only the foxes knew. It was quite a complex.

The Alpha met them in one of the forward rooms, near the mouth of the first cavern. She could see more openings leading off from there, and was intrigued, but there was no time to explore. First things first. She had to greet the Alpha on his home territory and make sure all the protocols were met. Tradition was very important to shifters and she wanted to be sure to adhere to it as much as possible, even in this time of crisis.

She also wanted to take the measure of the man her people had been dealing with. While she trusted their judgment, it was important to make her own decisions. The Nyx could trust no one implicitly—except maybe her mate. Ria took Jake's hand as they were ushered into the large room near the front of the cave system. He glanced at her, a question in his eyes, but she couldn't explain. Not now. It was enough that he was by her side. They would be partners from now on. She felt an immense sense of relief—coupled with a tiny bit of guilt—that she would no longer have to shoulder the burden of her position alone.

Ria gave Jake a smile, then turned to see the man waiting for them in the front room.

Not just a man, she quickly amended her thoughts. A man and his arsenal, apparently. She almost did a double take, but resisted. She knew her eyes had widened by the spark of humor in the man across the room's eyes. They were snapping golden eyes in a tanned face framed with—what else—red hair. The man was a fox, after all.

"Alpha, thank you for seeing us," Ria said, moving ahead, with Jake at her side. The sheer number of weapons in this room should have intimidated her, but in this particular instance, she was happy to see the foxes were well-armed for what might come.

She extended her hand and the fox did something surprising in one not of her own species. He moved in front of her and dropped to his knees, taking her hand in his and kissing the back of it lightly, sniffing her scent from her outstretched fingers. His eyes closed in what looked like relief mixed with joy for a moment as she puzzled out his response to her presence. She didn't meet a lot of other species all that often—especially not of the canine variety. Mostly she was surrounded by cats all the time and they were much more aloof, like their animal cousins.

The man rose to his feet and let go of her hand. His smile stretched from ear to ear.

"Forgive me, milady, I just never thought to meet the Nyx. I know it doesn't show on the outside, but my mother—the woman who raised me after finding me orphaned in the snow as a baby—was *tigre d'or*. She met your predecessor once and was told she would have a child, but in an unexpected way. She couldn't have cubs of her own, but when she came upon the scene of my parents' murder by hunters, she saved me, remembering the Nyx's words, and raised me as her own. So in a way, I have your predecessor to thank for being alive."

"Wow." There she went, being eloquent again. Ria almost kicked herself. She cleared her throat and tried again. "I'm glad my mother was able to give yours a message that helped you both. And now I understand what my mother told me last night," she thought out loud. Seeing the spark of interest in the man's golden eyes, she went on. "Last night during the new moon ceremony, I talked to my mother for the first time since she passed. She told me that things were coming full circle and that I would find allies among those whose lives had already been touched by the Nyx. I thought she meant my Royal Guard, but now I see she had an even deeper meaning in mind."

"Your mother was a great lady. I'm sorry for her loss," the fox Alpha said with deep respect in his tenor voice that brought a bit of a tear to her eye.

"Thank you, Alpha. She was the best and I'm glad she was able to touch your life in some small way. Your mother sounds like an amazing woman too."

The man grinned. "That she is. Now, please, call me Alan, and welcome to the McCoy Clan den. My people stand ready to assist you in any way we can."

It was almost too good to be true, but Ria didn't doubt the man's welcome one bit. Not when it was clear there were larger forces at work in this meeting than Ria could have imagined.

"Thank you, Alan. Call me Ria. And this is my mate, Jake," she introduced Jake, who had stood patiently at her side, watching the exchange.

The two men shook hands and though the fox Alpha was slightly shorter than Jake, he was every bit as powerful. This was a meeting of equals, regardless of the fact that Jake was human and the Alpha had all the advantages of an Alpha shifter. Fox or not, it was clear this guy, Alan McCoy, was a powerhouse.

"Quite a collection you have here," Jake said, making conversation as he looked around what had to be the Clan's armory.

Alan beamed. "We try to keep up with the latest technology. A number of my people are gunsmiths and weapons designers."

Ria could see that Jake was impressed as he whistled through his teeth. "I'm glad you're on *our* side."

Everyone chuckled at the truism and they were instantly on friendly footing.

Willard liked the way the other Council members looked at him after he made their latest plan work. There was no doubt that he had been the one wielding the combined power—and that was a lot—of the Council to raise the leviathan. Willard liked the evil creature, and it gave him a good idea for something he could do on land, as long as there was a body of water with fish in it available nearby.

He had been able to communicate with the creature when he broke through the final barrier behind which it had been trapped so long ago. It liked Willard for releasing it, and had given him a bit of knowledge in return for his help. The leviathan made it clear that was all Willard would get. The creature considered itself above the land-creatures' concerns and would not be controlled by any force presently in the mortal realm. It would do as it wished now that it was free and would answer to no man.

Willard was okay with that. The leviathan would serve its purpose. It would wreak havoc on the high seas and contribute to the end-of-the-world thinking among the human population of the earth. Better to get them used to the idea that dark times were coming. Elspeth would be here soon and she would show them the true meaning of the term *dark ages*.

And Willard would be by her side, a favored son for having rescued her from her exile.

One last parting gift from the leviathan would help make Willard's wet dream come true. The beast had told Willard exactly where he could find the Nyx.

CHAPTER EIGHT

A short while later, a contingent of Royal Guard moved in from the tree line, met by Dorian and Bronson, they were brought into the cave complex and introduced to the Alpha fox. After the formalities were taken care of with the local leader, the rather surprising leader of the beta team asked for a private audience with Ria.

She was a little shocked to see the man who took great pride in training her Royal Guard out on this mission, but then, Geir Falkes was a law unto himself. Never mated, Geir was a tiger shifter who had come to the *pantera noir* through marriage. His beloved aunt had married into the Clan and Geir had followed her from Iceland while still a young man, his own parents having died by the hand of the corrupt leader of the tigers who had recently been overthrown.

Geir had come out of the dojo where he trained the Guard to lead the beta team who had arrived as backup for Ria's four-person Guard team. The beta team consisted of all those who were still on active duty in Ria's service. She didn't require a lot of people to keep her safe, just a small team of four with her at all hours. When she had a home base, they usually split up the day into eight-hour shifts, so she would always be covered.

Her Royal Guard had been down a man or two since her

cousin Cade mated and settled down and his partner, Mitch, had raised hell over in Iceland, becoming the new tiger monarch. Geir had filled one of the empty spots by promoting young Bronson. The other two teams—seven in all—had gone ahead to prepare her next location while she made her way there with just the four Guards.

It took a lot of prep work to set up a new home base and lately they had been doing it every few weeks. Ria had been on the run for a long time, but in recent months it had gotten worse than ever. It was time to end that—here and now, if possible.

Ria and Jake, accompanied by her Guards went back to the cabin. Geir seemed to know Ben, and the two paired off to speak privately in the arsenal. When Ria and Jake arrived back at the cabin, the only people in it were members of her Guard. She was surrounded by *her* people and it felt really good to be home.

She had learned over the years of constantly traveling that home was where your loved ones were. It wasn't necessarily a fixed place. Wherever you happened to be, if you were with the people you loved, you were home.

Ria sat down at the central table, Jake at her side and finally felt a moment's peace. Things were looking up. She had her friends around her and support from unexpected sources. They just might prevail in the confrontation everything seemed to be pointing toward. They just had to live through the next few days and find a way to stop the *Venifucus* from winning.

"I'm so glad you're all here," Ria began. "Geir, thank you for coming. We can use your help. And for those of you who haven't met my mate yet, this is Jake. He's Cade's brother-in-law. Some of you may have met him at Mitch's wedding. Either way, he's part of our Clan now and he not only saved my life, but has given me hope for the future." She reached for his hand under the table.

"Congratulations, milady, and welcome to the Clan, Jake," Geir said formally. "I'm glad you've found happiness. I'm only sorry it had to happen at such a trying time." Geir's gaze narrowed on Jake, as if assessing him. "I've heard about your rescue at the warehouse, and I've asked around about you since then. From everything I've heard, I think we can work together, despite the differences in our training."

"You might be surprised how similar our training has been," Jake spoke up. "But I appreciate the sentiment, and the welcome, Master Geir." Geir's eyebrows rose at the use of his proper title and Ria had to stifle a chuckle.

Geir probably hadn't been able to find out too much about Jake's background—especially not the fact that he had trained with the secretive snowcats. In all likelihood, Geir was underestimating Jake's abilities, but he would learn. Hopefully he'd figure it out in time.

"Your friend Ben is an interesting fellow. Former *Altor Custodis* agent, isn't he? From everything I've been able to find he's changed his ways." There was an unspoken, doubt-filled *but* on the end of that sentence that made Jake frown. Geir was being polite, but he was expressing his uncertainty about at least one of the people Jake had brought into their inner circle.

"You can check with the Napa Valley Master Vampire if you like. Ben has done a lot of good things since he discovered the taint in the *AC*. He saw some things he shouldn't have down in South America while he was still in the service and discovered the existence of shifters and Others. The *AC* recruited him and he worked as an observer for them for a few years until he realized they were using his reports to target magical folk," Jake explained in a calm voice. "He's done his best to put things right since then and I have no doubts about his loyalty. He's a good man."

"So my friends who have worked with him say," Geir conceded, nodding to the original four Guards who had been with Ria since this escapade began.

It looked like he was about to argue when suddenly Jake went silent. Ria looked at him and realized something was happening. Another vision. Perhaps not as violent as the one on the yacht had been, but definitely enough to stop Jake in his tracks. She put her hand on his back, rubbing gently in comfort as he gripped the wooden arms of his chair until his knuckles went white.

"What's wrong?" Geir asked quietly, watching Jake with narrowed eyes.

"Unless I'm much mistaken, my *mate*..." she emphasized the word so there would be no misunderstanding of Jake's place in her life, "...is in the grips of a vision."

"Vision?" Geir repeated, his gaze going from Ria to Jake and back again. "So then the gossip is true. He's a seer?"

"Verified by no less than Sophia Grantham," Ria acknowledged, glad when Geir's attitude changed. She saw it in the respect and wariness that now filled his gaze. He had badly underestimated her mate and he was only beginning to realize it.

After a tense moment more, Jake shook his head and tried to refocus his gaze. He looked at her, coming out of the vision slowly, but much easier than the last time she'd witnessed something like this. She smiled at him, concern deep in her heart for him and what he might have seen.

"It's all right. You're okay, Jake. All is secure," she reassured him.

His expression hardened. "It won't be for long. The leviathan stirs and the battle is coming our way. I saw a circle of stones. That's where the battle will rage. It's where it *must* happen if our side has any hope of winning."

"When?" Ria asked, knowing they would camp out near the stone circle, if necessary.

"Tonight. At the height of the new moon."

Any reaction was smothered when the door to the cabin burst open, taking everyone within by surprise. It was Ben Steel.

"More new arrivals," he said in a clipped voice. "A tiger shifter and a couple of selkies are on their way up. Said it was urgent. They had to speak to you."

"Names?" Jake asked quickly.

"Tom Kinkaid. I think the other seal is his sister and the other guy said his name was Beau. Beau Champlain, maybe? Sounded like his voice on the radio, though I haven't seen him in years. He didn't give me a chance to ask before dropping the radio and stalking off through the woods, according to the fox scouts near the road."

"Sounds like him," Geir added with a smirk.

"Beau was on the yacht," Jake told them. "So was Tom. And he was in my vision. It's starting to make sense. We're going to need him and his sister. And the tiger." Jake's eyes shot to Geir. "Both of the tigers," he amended.

Geir held his tongue but bowed his head, holding Jake's gaze with respect. Ria was glad. It looked like all these powerful men were going to get along, which was a major step forward in securing everyone's safety.

The front door of the cabin opened a few minutes later to admit two men and a woman. Ria recognized the shifter who had met them when they landed on the yacht. She had thought he smelled of big cat, but he hadn't let her get close enough to know for sure. He had to be the tiger the scouts had mentioned. He looked a lot grouchier than the last time she'd seen him. A few of the men nodded to him as he walked through the small room to the table where Ria and Jake still sat with Geir. Ben stood nearby.

"Good to see you two still in one piece," he said gruffly as Jake stood and stretched out his hand to the other man.

"You made good time. The question is, why?" Jake asked. "I thought Edvard was running diversion, not sending his people straight here."

"Ask her." Beau pointed toward the petite woman coming up behind him as he stepped aside to make room for her and Tom Kinkaid, who walked with her.

Beau's temper was pretty close to the surface, Ria realized. He had been calm and collected—silent even—on the boat, but something had stirred his inner tiger and it practically growled out at them through his human voice.

"Please pardon Mr. Grumpy, milady," the young woman

said with a grimace as she walked slowly closer. "We had to come. Tante Sophia called and told me I had to reach you before tonight. It was of the utmost urgency. I asked Tom to help me get to you and Oscar the Grouch decided to tag along."

"Sophia Grantham sent you?" Geir asked the question that was on everyone's mind. "What did she say?"

"Only that I must be here to help guard the waters. Are there any waterways on this mountain?" She looked around as if trying to sense where there might be some hidden lake or pond.

"There's a stream and some waterfalls down the ridge a ways. Even a few swimming holes farther down the slope and a small lake up by the standing stones," Ben supplied. When everyone looked at him with varying degrees of surprise, he shrugged. "I talked to the foxes and hiked a bit. Wanted to get the lay of the land, since I don't have your shifter advantages."

Geir's eyebrow rose and he looked at his group of Guards as if to say, *why didn't you think of that?*

"We scouted around a little, but we only found the stream and the small lake up by the stone circle," Shelly admitted. Geir's expression alone was condemnation enough and the four Guard who had been here longest each looked chagrined at the reprimand from their teacher.

"All right then," Tom broke in to the heavy silence. "I know why we were sent here, but what can you do with Beau? I assumed an extra hand wouldn't come amiss."

"You've got that right." Jake rose to shake Tom's hand and offered the same friendly greeting to the young woman at Tom's side. They'd met her once before, on the yacht.

"This is my sister Jacki," Tom said for the benefit of everyone else present. "She's like me."

"Yeah, we figured," Geir admitted. "Ben said there were two selkies and a tiger on their way up."

Tom's brows drew together in a frown until Ben stepped in. "The foxes have a really keen sense of smell. The scout at the base of the mountain said—and I quote—that the guy and gal smelled like seaweed and the big-ass tiger was on the warpath."

Ria couldn't help it. She laughed, and so did everyone else—even Beau cracked a grudging smile as Tom slapped his back. Finally, something to smile about in this harrowing situation. It couldn't last, but it felt good to have even this small thing to laugh at for a brief moment.

Jake looked out the window, noting the angle of the sun. The afternoon was upon them and soon it would be night. They had several hours yet. His vision showed the time of the confrontation to be somewhere around midnight. But he didn't want to see this day pass so quickly. It might be the last day they had.

"I think everyone's here that we need to be here right now," Jake said, calling the room to attention. "What I just saw changes things. The attack is going to come tonight. It makes sense. Tonight is the midpoint of the new moon, right?" He looked at Ria for confirmation.

"Technically, the new moon is tonight, yes. But I'm able to reach those beyond for three nights—the day before, the day of the new moon, and the day after," she answered. "The connection will be strongest tonight."

"Which is what they're counting on," Jake replied, picking up the thread of the conversation. "The *Venifucus* want to use the Nyx's power to infiltrate the veil between realms and bring back their leader from exile." Grim faces all around met this statement. "They're going to try tonight, when your connection is strongest. The standing stones will offer us some protection, but there are drawbacks to the location. The waterways aren't safe as long as the *Venifucus* is stirring up evil creatures from the depths."

"But we're over five thousand feet above sea level," Dorian hopefully pointed out.

"Doesn't matter," Jake insisted. "They have a lot of magic on their side—and not the good kind. Water is their domain for now. It has to be suspect." He looked almost apologetically at the brother and sister seal shifters.

"We'll take the water," Tom said. "It's pretty obvious that's why we were sent here."

"There's a small lake and then there's a stream leading from it that trickles down the mountain, making a semi-circle around the lower half of the stone circle," Ben supplied helpfully.

"I've got the lake," Tom said at once, his gaze daring his sister to argue.

"I'll watch over the stream, then," she agreed, though she clearly wasn't happy about it, from the angry spark in her eyes.

"And I'll back them both up," Beau volunteered. "I've been working with selkies a lot lately," he explained. "And tigers love the water." He seemed almost embarrassed by the attention, but he was sticking by what he'd said.

"I will stand with you," Geir said unexpectedly. "Two tigers are always better than one." Geir winked, of all things, and Jake just had to shake his head at whatever silent messages were being sent and received between them.

It wasn't Jake's place to nose into whatever the tigers and the selkies had going on, but it was pretty clear there was something strange happening there. Maybe Jacki was at the center of it? Jake wasn't sure—and he wasn't sure he even wanted to know.

"So that squares away the tigers and seals," Jake forged ahead. "Now the question is, what are we going to do with the rest of you?"

He looked around the room and realized they were missing three very important pieces of the puzzle. Ben had brought in three more operatives who were somewhere on the mountain. They needed to be in on this. Jake nodded at Ben.

"Where are your guys?" Jake asked his human friend.

Ben didn't speak, just nodded over Jake's shoulder. Jake turned and was dumbfounded to find there were three more shifters in the room. They had to have come in the back door at some point, but Jake hadn't heard them arrive. Nor, it seemed had Ria, who turned with him. He saw the way her eyes widened. Only Geir and the folks who had been facing the back of the room seemed unsurprised to find three more heavily armed soldiers in woodland camo ranged along the back wall of the cabin.

One of the men moved forward, taking point. He stopped before Ria and bowed with a slight flair of the east to his movements. Jake started to realize who he was, but the man introduced himself to Ria, saving Jake the trouble.

"It is my honor to greet the lady of the *pantera noir*," the somewhat suave soldier stated. "I am Seth. Some call me The Golden Jackal."

Ria's eyes widened and Jake realized the mercenary's reputation had preceded him. Everyone in military circles—especially those in on the secret world of shifters—knew about The Golden Jackal. But exactly what they knew, varied greatly from person to person. Jake had always suspected that was something Seth encouraged.

The Jackal, it was said, was originally from Turkey, but he spoke many languages and usually worked for the highest bidder. He was the leader of a band of mercenaries, which was the best that could be said for his ragtag group of heavily armed followers.

The only thing that set The Jackal apart from others of his ilk, was that he was rumored to actually have a conscience. It was said that he would only take on causes that he believed were just—however he defined that term. If there was such a thing as honor among thieves, The Golden Jackal actually had some.

"I've heard of you," Ria replied, offering her hand. Seth took her hand in his, bowing over it, kissing the back and sniffing delicately. The sniffing was a shifter thing but Jake still didn't like the expression on Seth's face when he looked at Ria. The suave bastard.

When Seth rose he gestured somewhat theatrically to the

men behind him. One of the hulking brutes came up on either side of The Jackal. It was pretty obvious that the two men were related, though they seemed to be opposite sides of the same coin.

One had light hair. The other had dark hair. One had blue eyes. The other had green. One was scarred. The other looked unblemished. But both carried their weapons, and themselves, with authority. And after a moment, Jake realized he had met these two before, a long time ago.

"Pax and Ari Rojas?" Jake asked, trying to recall the details of his first, and only, encounter with the twin behemoths.

Identical smiles spread over nearly identical faces. The men were indeed twins, but of the fraternal variety. Still, they shared many characteristics with each other. And they were both jaguar shifters, if Jake remembered correctly.

Seth stepped back and allowed the brothers to kneel before Ria's turned chair, making their bows over her hand. They were silent until the formalities had been observed and they were both back on their feet.

"It's good to see you again, sir," Pax said to Jake.

"Our Clan affiliation is the Arizona Jaguar Clan, though we haven't been home in a while," Ari admitted to Ria. "We're at your service, milady."

"I'm glad to have you here," Ria replied politely, her smile genuine. The Rojas brothers were men of few words usually, and they both seemed quite taken with Ria.

Jake reached out and took her hand in his, making their relationship a bit clearer to the newcomers. He wasn't normally a jealous man, but something about mating Ria was causing all sorts of caveman thoughts to race through his mind. She squeezed his hand as if she understood and the Rojas brothers didn't miss the subtle byplay.

Jake tried hard to regain some equilibrium. Best to concentrate on the matter at hand. They had a mission to plan. Things had changed. He'd seen things about tonight and knew their original plans would have to be altered. They were running out of time. Things had to start happening now if they were going to have any chance of pulling out a victory.

Jake stood and moved to the side of the room so he could see everyone. The brothers backed off to give him room to maneuver, for which he was grateful. Every step they took away from Ria calmed his inner caveman a little more.

"All right. Those of you who are deadlier in your fur, use that to your advantage. Everybody else, we have the Mount Sterling Ridge fox Clan's incomparable arsenal at our disposal. Take what you can use and use what you take. The toys are on loan only, but the ammo is ours to distribute at will." Jake paused to try to put some order to his thoughts. "I've seen the battle to come and it's not going to be easy. Fur will fly and it's possible there could be a threat from the water, which is where our selkie and tiger friends come in. The rest of you... Royal Guards, do what you do best. Surround your queen inside the stone circle and defend her with your lives if necessary. Ben, Seth and the Rojases, I want you outside the circle of stones. In fact, I need a few snipers. Figure out among yourselves who will fill that role best and since Ben seems to know the land better than everyone but the foxes, he can help figure out where to place our nests."

"Cats don't nest," Bronson murmured loud enough for Jake to hear him.

"Snipers do," Jake replied without breaking stride. "We should try to make this look good to draw in our enemy. If we can catch them between the outer defenders and the inner circle, we might be able to end this quickly. So I'm going to ask Ria to pretend to do a new moon ceremony inside the sacred circle. Have some of your people pretend to be asking for guidance, that sort of thing." The Royal Guards nodded and Jake decided to leave the assignment of roles up to them. "The fox scouts will be on the outermost perimeter and will warn us when the enemy is on their way. They're going to be our eyes and ears until we're ready to spring the trap."

Nods of agreement met this plan all around the room. Jake was pleased, but didn't give them any time to pose questions. Time was running out.

"Ben, do you have an ETA on Moore's men?" Jake asked.

Ben didn't look pleased. "Not for a while yet, last I heard. They've gone dark, Jake. They're in transit. That's all I know."

Jake cursed inwardly. "We'll just have to hope they show up in time for the party."

CHAPTER NINE

Ria called a halt to the meeting after they had hashed out everything they could hash out and a quick meal had been consumed. The fox Alpha had sent over some of his people with trays of sandwiches and drinks. It wasn't grand, but it was fuel their bodies needed to perform at peak efficiency.

In small groups of three or four, each of them went over to the fox arsenal and came back armed with additional weapons, some large, some small, but all lethal. Ria was persuaded to add to the weapons Edvard had given them before they left the yacht. She knew how to use everything from small arms to bazookas, but she was most comfortable with pistols and blades, so that's what she kitted herself out with.

On the way back, she paused before leaving the cave, one hand on Jake's forearm. She wasn't sure how to tell him what she wanted, but she figured honesty was probably the best policy.

"How much time do we have?" she asked, stalling even though she'd decided to come clean.

"A few hours. Why?" Jake turned to look at her with concern in his eyes. She loved how attentive he was to her. Maybe that would fade with time and familiarity, but right now, it made her feel cherished in a way she hadn't ever experienced. It felt really good.

"Um…I've been two-legged for quite a while now. I was wondering if I could get in a short run before everything hits the fan. It might help me focus. The cat needs a stretch." She watched him carefully to see how he would handle this evidence of her animal side. He hadn't ever seen her cat and she was a little worried at how he would react. "You don't have to come if you would rather not," she added quickly, turning away, chickening out rather than face the possibility of his disapproval.

But Jake grabbed her arm lightly, stopping her retreat. She turned around again, but wouldn't look at him until he tilted her head up with one gentle finger under her chin. She met his eyes, worried…but she shouldn't have doubted him. Jake's gaze was full of understanding…and excitement.

"Are you kidding me? Sweetheart, I've been dying to see what you look like in your fur. I bet you're gorgeous. Exotic, athletic, soft and yet deadly. Everything I love about you, amplified by four paws. Just try to leave me behind—though come to think of it, you're probably a hell of a lot faster than I am when you've got four feet and the musculature to power them." He tugged her toward the cave entrance. "Come on. Ben told me about a place and we can do some in-person recon while we're at it."

"You really don't mind?" His reaction was almost too good to be true. How had she found a mate who was so understanding of her differences and even enthusiastic about her abilities that might be just that much better than his, as a human? The Goddess had surely been smiling on her when She brought them together.

"Mind?" Jake laughed. "Honey, I know it's early days for us yet, but please try to have a little faith. There is nothing about you that I could ever *mind*." He emphasized the word with a roll of his eyes, then he leaned down and kissed her right in front of everyone and anyone who might be able to see them near the cave entrance. "You're the other half of my soul, Ria," he breathed as he let go of their kiss. "Everything about you is perfect." He moved away and grinned. "Me, on the other hand...well...I don't pretend to be perfect, but I suppose you'll get used to my bad habits over time. You could always swat me with your tail when I leave the toilet seat up or my dirty socks on the floor."

"Or if you really screw up, don't forget I have claws," she joked, running her fingernails lightly down his arm.

"Ouch." He laughed with her and what she had thought would be a problem practically disappeared.

Though they still had to get through the shift and she would be watching him carefully to see if he truly didn't mind that she could go furry and he couldn't. Her biggest fear right now was that he would be disgusted by the process—or the result. It wasn't the most graceful thing to become another form.

Jake led her up the mountainside and they both looked around carefully as they went along. He made a few comments about defensible positions and cover that made her think a bit harder about the terrain they were passing. Jake taught as if he already knew what was going to happen tonight —and he probably did. He'd seen the battle ahead and she was pretty certain he hadn't told them everything he'd seen.

That worried her, but she figured he had his reasons. She wondered how he decided what to disclose about the future and what to keep quiet. If they were given more time together—if they both survived the battle to come—she would enjoy learning more about his gift and how he had learned to deal with it all.

She felt the energy of the place change and realized they had arrived at the circle of stones. It was small and hidden from the air by the tops of the trees, which bowed over the circle as if in benediction. The power of the place called to her and she felt the amulet around her neck stir to life. Being inside the circle later tonight would really be something.

She usually didn't find herself in places of power during the new moon rituals. The few times she had, the experiences had been memorable. The circle would amplify the effect of the amulet, which probably wasn't the greatest idea. But by the same token, the circle of stones and their Light energy would protect her and the amulet like no other place.

"What is it?" Jake must have picked up on her internal conflict.

"I was just thinking about tonight. This place..." she gestured to the stone circle in front of them. "It'll be both the safest place for me and the most dangerous."

"How so?" His brows drew together in concern.

"The stones could make the effect of the new moon stronger, but they'll also protect anything within the circle more than any other place. The Lady's protections are strong here and She will look after Her servants—or so the priestesses always say. I can only hope they're right in this case."

Jake looked as if he wasn't sure how to answer. "I did see something..." He trailed off, but she waited for him to go on. "I saw you here, and something very powerful happening. I won't lie to you—this could still go either way, and I won't taint your response by telling you anything that might not be helpful in the long run. Do you trust me?"

She didn't even have to think about that one. "Of course."

"Then trust me on this one. Things might start to look bad at times, but I think I've seen enough to know how to make this end in our favor." He moved closer, tugging her into his arms for a hug.

"And if it doesn't work out that way?" she asked in a small voice, not happy to think about losing him—losing everything—but needing to be realistic.

"And if it doesn't work out, then at least we'll have given it our best shot. We won't have given up or given in. We'll have stood strong for as long as we possibly could. You've been strong for so long, Ria. Don't give up on me now." He kissed her again, waiting until she responded to his kiss with more enthusiasm. The man had a way about him that could coax her out of her blackest moods.

"You're a charming so-and-so, Jake. I'm glad you came to my rescue and I'm glad you're my mate. I can't imagine a more perfect mate for me." She rested her head over his heart, reveling in the stolen moment out of time.

"Ditto, sweetheart," he whispered as he held her for one what was probably minutes, but felt like a wonderful eternity. She wanted forever with this man and would do everything and anything in her power to make that happen.

At length, he let her go, keeping one arm around her shoulders as he guided her away from the stone circle and toward a destination only he knew. She walked silently with him, seeing the woods through his eyes as he continued to make note of various features of the terrain.

Jake led her to a magical glade just below the stone circle and off to one side. It was sheltered on all sides by towering trees, but in the middle of the small space made by the trees, there was a blanket of moss that had to be a couple of inches thick. Lush and green, it was springy and inviting under her feet.

"Will this do for a place to shift to your four-footed form?" Jake asked, watching her reaction to the special place. She nodded, already taking off her coat and kicking off her shoes. "I wanted my memory of the first time I saw you in your fur to be special," Jake whispered, his voice a low rumble that stirred her senses. He moved closer, reaching for the hem of her sweater, taking it from her grasp. "Allow me."

Jake took over the task of undressing her, which slowed the process, but she wasn't complaining. He stroked his strong hands over her sensitive skin, taking her down to her underwear...and then continuing until she was completely bare.

"Have I told you how gorgeous you are?" Jake's rumbling tone made her shiver all over.

"A girl can never hear that enough, I think," she replied playfully. "Are you ready for this?" She wanted to give him time to prepare for what was coming.

"Ready as I'll ever be. Come on, sweetheart. I promise not

to laugh."

"Laugh? I'll give you something to laugh about." Her inner cat was outraged, but as she shifted form into the cat, she realized maybe that's what he'd been hoping for. His distraction worked to quell her nerves and she shifted shape in a shimmer of dark light that left the cat behind as the woman receded.

A low whistle issued from Jake's lips as he looked at her. She shifted her weight nervously on her front paws, watching for his reaction. But he didn't make her wait long. He crouched down so their eyes were on the same level and he grinned slowly, invitingly. She moved forward, rubbing her head against his cheek.

The cat knew its mate, as did the woman, and when his hands came up to stroke over her fur, she reveled in the touch of her lover. His fingers knew just how to stroke her, petting her in ways that made the cat purr.

"Oh, honey, you are beautiful," he whispered near her ear, which twitched, wanting to catch every nuance of his tone. The cat read honesty in the subtleties of pitch and timbre only it could discern.

They stayed there for a long moment, his hands rubbing over her in slow waves of possession that made her chest rumble with delight. She felt his smile against her fur and she rubbed all over him, wanting her scent on his body, his clothing. She even licked his hair, which made him laugh. Then he stood.

"I believe you said something about a run?" he challenged. "I won't claim to be able to keep up, but I'll come along, if you don't mind and keep watch while you nose around, okay?"

She liked that plan and nodded her head once before setting off. He jogged through the trees while she bounded to the sides of his path and back again, giving her legs a good, long stretch. She ran ahead, then came back, then paced with him, guiding his steps with subtle shoves against his legs until he figured out where she wanted to go.

Eventually their steps led them back to the stone circle, which seemed to be calling to her even more strongly now. She followed her instincts, which were driving her to enter the circle, where she hadn't before.

She prowled inside the sheltering circle of monolithic granite stones. They glistened in the dim light under the trees with mystery and invitation. The place welcomed her and she made a quick round from stone to stone, enjoying the energy surge as each ancient stone seemed to welcome her presence.

The stones were tall and rugged, standing like guardians around the central cleared space. The trees sheltered the grassy area below, reaching their branches out and over, hiding the circle for the most part, so it couldn't be seen from the air—unless one knew what to look for. And in the center of the stone circle was a smooth, flat rock that pulsed with magical, blessed energy.

Ria was drawn to it, allowing her front paw to touch, tentatively. She wasn't all that surprised to find that the giant, square, table-shaped stone was warm, not cold as it should be. The power of the place hummed through it, thrumming against the pads of her feet as she investigated. She sniffed with her cat nose, but this was more a phenomenon that had to be felt. Her human hands were better for that purpose, so she shifted to two legs to continue her investigation.

She wasn't surprised to feel Jake come up behind her. Thick, strong fingers swept around her waist, then one hand slid upward to cup her breast, while the other went downward, to insinuate itself between her thighs. His mouth was at her neck and she was powerless against the surge of desire that swept through her body.

It felt like her arousal was supercharged by the energy of the altar stone. She felt her body responding to Jake's slightest touch. She wanted him. Now.

"You are the sexiest woman alive," he whispered, his teeth tugging gently at her earlobe. Her cat purred and the sound came through her chest, startling her a bit.

Only Jake could cause that response. Only Jake—her true

mate—could make her purr in human form. The cat liked the way he stroked their skin. And it just plain loved the scent and taste of him. He'd done well, allowing her the freedom to run where the cat willed, but being ready to protect and just be with her even though he couldn't shapeshift. The cat liked his willingness to accept her altered form and wanted to show its appreciation for the acceptance and love she had felt while in cat form.

No time like the present. Especially when Jake's fingers moved into her folds, sliding in the warm juices her body was producing for him. She squirmed in his arms, loving the feel of his strength surrounding her.

"Then we're a good match," she whispered back, turning just her head to brush his lips with hers. "Because you're the sexiest man alive."

He made a sound that was halfway between a chuckle and a growl. It turned her on. Big time. Not that she needed any help in that direction. Between his hands stroking over her body—one tugged at her nipples, switching from one to the other every so often, and the other one was currently rubbing little circles around her clit—and the power of the sacred place, she was going up in flames already and they'd barely begun.

"I need you inside me." She was going to beg in a minute, if he didn't get a move on.

He stilled behind her. "Right now?"

"Five minutes ago," she replied, her breath hitching as she felt his dick rubbing against her ass through is pants. She wanted that piece of hard, thick male flesh inside her—and she wanted it now.

"Are you sure?" His words were definitely a growl this time and the animalistic sound coming from his purely human body made her want to bite him—in a really good way.

"Now, Jake," she replied, her voice a demanding whisper. There might've been a hint of a growl in there too, come to think of it. The cat wanted to be scratched in just the right way—the way only Jake knew.

"Your wish is my command, milady." She pouted when his hands moved away from her body, but she heard the zip of his pants, followed by a rustle of fabric, and then he was back. His cock nudged her ass with no fabric between them now and she wanted to sing.

In fact, she did make some joyful noise when he bent her over the altar stone and pushed inside her, slow and steady. She loved that he was taking care, even when she was demanding he join with her in what must seem like extreme haste. But her need of him was far from hasty. With Jake, she seemed always to be ready for him, always willing, always able.

And with the power of the altar stone flowing through her, she was even going beyond her usual thresholds. She wanted everything he had to give. And more. A lot more.

He began to thrust and she reached for the stone, holding herself against it so that her breasts wouldn't scrape along the rough surface. At least—not too hard. And not all the time. The small amount of contact that happened, only made her desire spike higher as Jake's pace started slow and increased by small amounts as time went on.

She screamed when her first climax hit and she knew it was only the beginning.

"Are you okay?" Jake had stopped moving, though he stayed within her.

"I'm good," she gasped. "Keep going!"

"I don't want to hurt you," he whispered against her neck. He was bent over her as she rested for a moment against the surface of the warm stone.

"It'll only hurt if you stop," she insisted.

He withdrew and turned her around so that her butt rested against the altar stone. She lay back as he joined with her again, driving slow and steady until her body began to quiver in anticipation of another, higher climax. She reached for him, guiding him as they came together this time, a whiplash of power binding them on the altar and to each other.

It was profound. It was sacred. It was the most amazing thing she had ever felt. Their two souls, bound in this sacred place, never to be parted.

Jake groaned as he came, his body covering hers completely as they both reached the pinnacle together. The stone pulsed with energy beneath her shoulders and probably under his palms if he was sensitive to such things. She thought maybe he was. He was magical too—in his own way.

There were no words to speak about the magical, intensely intimate thing that had just happened between them. Ria collapsed under him as he moved off, just a bit to the side so he wouldn't crush her and they lay there, limbs entwined, in the Lady's sacred circle for a few minutes while they caught their breath.

They didn't talk. The power of the place was too overwhelming for mere words. It affected them both. It wasn't long before she felt Jake's cock stir. In fact, she wasn't far behind. The energy of the altar stone thrummed through her, reigniting the fire she thought had just been banked. Apparently the stone circle—or perhaps the Lady—had other ideas.

But Ria was all for it. If this was her last day in the mortal realm, she wanted to spend as much time enjoying her mate as she could. They'd had precious little time together alone since discovering each other. Things had been happening too fast. Danger had followed their every step. This little interlude seemed like the only time they might have and she wanted to make the most of it.

Either one of them—or both—could die this night. She didn't want to leave behind too many regrets if she had to pass through the veil. Nor did she want Jake to leave her alone in this lonely mortal realm. Now that she had found him, she never wanted to be parted from him.

That thought made her cling to him, clutching at his shoulders when he moved to lever himself up off the stone. He paused, meeting her gaze.

"Don't go," she whispered.

He made soothing, shushing sounds and leaned in to kiss her gently and with such care, it brought tears to her eyes. She loved him so much. And if his actions were any indication, he cared as deeply for her, though he hadn't yet spoken the words. Perhaps he never would. Some shifter men took it for granted that their mate would understand everything mating entailed—physically and emotionally.

But Jake was human. She bit her lower lip, worrying about something she couldn't come straight out and ask him. Normally, she wouldn't hesitate to pose any question she wanted, but this was something he had to come forward with first. He had to make the first move or she might never feel the words were valid.

Time, she counseled herself. If they had the time, everything would work out. And if it turned out they didn't have the time, what did it really matter anyway? The only thing that should matter was these stolen moments. Right now. That's all they had and that's all she should be worrying about.

She wrapped one hand around the nape of his neck as he drew back from the kiss. "Make love to me again," she begged in a soft whisper that didn't intrude on the sanctity of the space.

"Are you sure?" Jake seemed uncertain though she could feel the evidence of his desire against her leg.

He wanted her. That much was obvious. But he was being a gentleman. The realization brought more emotion welling up within her. He was such a sweet man, though she was sure he would never agree to such a word being applied to himself.

There was only one answer to her mate. "Yes."

A spark ignited behind his eyes and she felt the heat in his touch as he began to stroke her body with strong, knowing hands. He took his time, touching every inch of her bare skin, following his fingers with kisses and little, exciting nibbles her inner cat enjoyed immensely.

She was squirming on the altar stone once more within a

few minutes, ready for him again. But Jake had different ideas this time. He moved her so that he sat on the stone, and guided her hips so that she sat above, straddling him. He smiled up at her, giving her control.

"Do your worst, milady," he quipped and she had to grin. She loved it when he dominated her, but she also liked to take control occasionally. Here was her perfect mate, giving her what she needed. The Goddess really did know what She was doing when she designed them for each other.

She began to make love to him, holding his gaze as his eyes sparked in that sexy way he had. He really was a magical, mysterious man and she would enjoy the years to come—if they were granted any—learning all his secrets and letting him learn hers. They were well matched if these few days were anything to go by. He seemed to know what she wanted even before she knew herself.

She balanced with her hands on his chest for a moment, enjoying the feel of him sliding deep inside her. She began to move, slowly at first, acclimating herself to the feel of him all over again. Once she had a rhythm going, she felt the fire inside her burn hotter, driving her to more motion, more intensity, more…everything.

Her head dropped back and she closed her eyes as she rode him, just feeling. It was so incredibly intense, so hot, so perfect. Jake's hands went to her hips, steadying her as a small climax hit. Her body bucked, but it wanted more. The little orgasm didn't let her stop to rest. Her body demanded more and a keening cry left her lips, moving upward through the trees.

"Look at me, Ria." Jake's harsh voice rasped over her senses, not to be denied.

Her head dropped forward and her eyes opened. His gaze swirled with energy and passion that nearly stole her breath. She felt her own magic rising up to answer the call, swirling around her body, sensitizing every last inch of her skin. Something really special was happening here. Something epic.

And then a twig snapped. Ria stilled immediately, looking

around the sheltering stones.

Then she saw them. Two men. Light and dark. Two sides of the same coin.

The Rojas brothers.

They were watching her make love to her mate and their strong jaws were set in tight lines. They looked almost as if they were in pain, but she understood. The cat inside her knew that look and reveled in the fact that they could watch, but not participate. She had her chosen mate already. She didn't need two jaguars—mighty as they were. She had the only man she wanted beneath her.

But that didn't mean the cat didn't enjoy their attention.

Ria's breath caught as another little climax took her by surprise. She looked down at Jake and she saw knowledge in his eyes. He knew! Or he had known they would come. She realized he might've seen this very scenario in one of his visions. The cretin, she thought with a little inward grin. The least he could've done was warn her.

Ria hadn't known she had any exhibitionist tendencies, but she was a shifter, after all. And shifters did it in the woods—in their fur and out of it—and often didn't care who saw them. It was part of being what they were. Part of the animal nature that shared their souls.

Catching her breath, Ria looked back at the two men. Pax, and his brother, Ari, she recalled. They were both handsome in a solid, jaguar sort of way. Sinuous. Sleek. Tall and strong. Mysterious. She looked down at their pants and the respective bulges barely contained by the fabric. And hard. Very hard, indeed.

She smiled at first one, then the other brother, nodding toward their crotches and she wasn't disappointed when they followed her unspoken invitation and lowered their zippers. Two hard cocks sprang out, into waiting hands.

The brothers formed a triangle to her and Jake, who were still on the altar stone. Pax was off to their left, just behind and to the left of the northwestern standing stone, and his brother, Ari, was to their right, just to the right of the northeastern stone. They probably couldn't see each other clearly, but they both had an unobstructed view of her and her lover on the altar stone.

Ria began to move again, her body undulating in sultry waves as she put on a bit of a show that heightened her own pleasure. She could tell that Jake liked it too. His hands guided her, lifting her up high so her pussy was clearly displayed, his cock sliding almost all the way out before she plunged back down, accepting him greedily.

She watched the Rojas brothers stroke themselves as they watched her body accept her mate over and over. She realized within moments that she was in control of three men's pleasure in that instant. The Rojas men and her mate would come when she wanted them to, and no sooner. It was a heady thought.

For a woman who'd had next to no sex life for years, she was certainly making up for lost time. Ria had never thought of herself as a femme fatale, but she found she liked the idea. She liked it a lot.

Her body began that incredible quiver that she had come to recognize as a sign that an incredible orgasm was very near. She hated to end this interlude, but her body would not be denied—and she'd kept the men on the cusp of coming for long enough, she figured. They deserved a little relief too.

She reached down and spread her inner lips, displaying herself to the men, circling her clit with one finger while she slammed down on Jake's cock with hard, fast digs that sent her senses soaring. She nodded at Ari, then Pax, her slight signal giving them leave to come in hard bursts, their thick, white ropes of come shooting into the stone circle, bathing the ground in front of them each with the stuff of life, a blessing of a kind for a Goddess that was known as the Mother of All.

Ria cried out when she came and Jake was only a split second behind, shooting deep inside her, filling her to overflowing as she collapsed on top of him. He held her as their breathing sounded through the circle, four souls trying hard to catch their breath from an experience unlike anything she ever could have expected.

She craned her neck, stretching to look over toward the brothers. They each leaned heavily on the standing stone they were next to, clearly moved and a little wrung out by what they had all just experienced. It was as if the stone circle had demanded their participation, using the pure, sexual energy of the moment to recharge itself against the coming trials.

If so, Ria couldn't think of a better use of their time. Or maybe it was just her fanciful thinking. Maybe she was just really horny now that she had a mate to make love to any time she wanted. Either way, the experience had been profound.

She lay her head back down on Jake's shoulder and let him soothe her into a light doze. His hands stroked over her back and lulled her into a feeling of complete peace. It was the most serene feeling she had ever experienced as an adult, and a moment to treasure.

But all too soon, they had to get up. Jake didn't seem to want to let her go, nor did she want to leave this idyllic place, but they both knew their duty and what they had to do to prepare. As she hopped off the altar stone, Ria looked toward the north, unsurprised to find both Rojas brothers gone. They had left as silently as they'd arrived, and with as little fanfare.

Ria and Jake walked back to the mossy glade, sharing the sounds of the forest in a companionable silence. When they got to where they had left her clothes, Jake spun her into his arms and kissed her. Things escalated and before she really knew what she was doing, she had unfastened his pants and pushed them away. His cock was hard and ready again. And she was just as ready.

Jake paused, his hard cock between her eager thighs.

"Did that get you hot, Ria? Making three men come for you?" Jake's harsh whisper dared her to admit the truth. She pulled back to look into his eyes and what she saw there enflamed her even further.

"Yes," she moaned as he drove into her in one long, hard glide.

"Did you like being watched?" He demanded, still in that sultry whisper that drove her wild. He began to thrust in earnest, her body shaking in heated response. "Did you like being the center of three guys' hottest fantasy?"

She could only moan as his pace increased. Jake might not be a shifter, but he had more than his share of agility and stamina. He rode her hard and left her crying out for more. He touched her deep and hard, just the way she liked it. He gave her all and demanded everything in return.

"I'll let them watch," Jake gritted out. "But I'll never let another man touch you. Are you okay with that?" His words were hard and fast, like his thrusts into her body.

She nodded. "I...only want...you," she gasped as he drove her senses higher with each tempestuous move.

"Poor bastards. They'll never know how truly amazing you are, Ria." He leaned down and kissed her, then moved his mouth to her neck, baring his teeth in a way that made her want to scream.

It wasn't unheard of for shifters to bite or claw during sex, but Ria had never really been interested in pain. Still, she had to admit, something primitive in her loved the feel of his teeth on her skin. When he nipped, she squeaked in pleasure. When he bit, she rocketed to the stars.

The cat screeched inside her head, signaling her approval. The cat liked it rough, apparently, and now, so did Ria. But only with Jake. No other man would ever touch her again and there was a sense of pride and possessiveness that filled her just thinking about the mating bond that had formed between them.

"Are you ready?" Jake asked her, his voice rough.

She could feel his body tensing and she found an answering tension in her own muscles, even though she'd just come. Only Jake had ever made her respond so readily. For him, she could come pretty much on command...and didn't that thought set off a whole new set of shivers in her pleasure centers.

"Yes!" she gasped, wanting to find the stars again in his arms. Wanting to be possessed as fully as she could be. Wanting to be his, and his alone.

"Then come with me now, baby," Jake ground out as he pounded into her once, twice, and then a third and final time before they exploded into ecstasy together. As one.

CHAPTER TEN

They rested for a few minutes on the mossy ground, but all too soon, Jake knew, they had to get dressed and go back. The time for action was almost upon them. Night was falling hard under the trees.

"Are you okay?" he asked gently, stroking her back as she lay against him on the soft ground. He'd pushed her pretty hard just now and he wasn't quite sure what was fine in the heat of passion would still be all right when saner heads prevailed.

She rose up, resting her chin on his chest while she met his gaze at an awkward angle. But even so, he could see her gaze was lazy and loving…and supremely satisfied. He felt an answering echo in his own body. Maybe he shouldn't have worried. It looked like his lady was on board with the kinky desires he hadn't quite known he'd had before now.

"I'm spectacular," she answered, drawing out each syllable. "And you are pretty spectacular too." She looked at him a moment more, then rose higher, comfortable in her nudity, stretching like the cat she was as she looked around the enchanted glade. "I guess we have to get back, huh?" Her expression fell just a bit. "It's a shame. I would've liked to spend an eternity or two right here, making love with you, but as usual, duty calls and I must answer."

He caught her hand as she started to move away and she looked over her shoulder at him.

"But this time, you're not alone." He waited, feeling their heartbeats draw out the time. One beat, then two. "You'll never be all on your own again, Ria. Not while I live."

Her smile broadened, even as a tear fell from her eye. "It's a wonderful thing, having a mate. And even more wonderful that my mate is you, Jake." She leaned in and kissed him, long and delicate, as if sealing their bond.

But all too soon, she drew away and even though he wanted to draw her back into his arms, he knew he couldn't. Time was not on their side right now. They'd managed to steal a couple of precious hours away from all the craziness that had overtaken their lives, but now they had to rejoin the battle and be on their toes.

All in all, he thought taking the time out was a good thing. This little interlude had drawn them closer together, cementing their relationship in the physical sense and helping them get to know more about each other emotionally too. Being with his mate could never be considered a bad thing, but if they had to face danger together tonight, he was glad he could at least give her pleasure before they had to do the really difficult stuff.

"I love you, Ria," he stated, needing her to know what was in his heart before they faced down evil together.

Ria paused. She had been getting dressed, but she stilled, turning slightly to look at him. She had a bit of the deer-in-the-headlights look on her face and he wasn't quite sure if that was good or bad until she spoke.

"I..." She seemed to fumble for words for a moment while he sweated. He didn't understand all the nuances of shifter mating. Maybe he'd made a misstep? Should he not have spoken of feelings? Was he only supposed to focus on the animal attraction? He just didn't know.

"Jake, I love you too," she finally got out, her voice breathy. "Forgive me. I wasn't sure..." She trailed off again, but he gave her time to collect her thoughts and find the right words. "I didn't know if you would feel the same things a shifter feels for their mate because you're human, but when I felt the bond…"

"You mean that energy bolt that hit us on the altar?" He had to laugh even as he stood to search for his jeans. He was both thrilled and a little uncomfortable with the words he'd somehow felt compelled to blurt out. "I felt that, Ria. Like lightning down my spine that went from me to you and back again. It drew us closer than I've ever been to anyone in my life."

"The mating bond." Her grin was full of wonder and pleased happiness. "I never realized it would be so intense. Then again, the location we chose to seal our troth could have had something to do with it." She chuckled and continued dressing. "Or you could just be the most amazing lover in the history of the universe. I haven't decided."

"I'd go with number two, but if you need more convincing, I'm up for that anytime you want, baby." He winked at her, getting into the spirit of their teasing as they put on their clothing.

It was a little rumpled and there were a few stray leaves and pine needles here and there, but they were presentable soon enough. They were arm in arm as they headed back down to the cabin, under the deepening cover of the trees.

The Rojas brothers flanked them and Ria only blushed a little when she caught sight of them, but the men were all business. They had their hands on their weapons—the metal ones this time—and were guarding Ria's descent to the cabin with serious intent. They were good men and although Jake hadn't planned the admittedly kinky scene that had happened up at the stone circle, he didn't regret it. Ria's response had made it clear that their presence was something unexpected and amazingly hot for her—and Jake was in the business now of giving Ria anything and everything she didn't even know she wanted.

He started to think about things he could introduce her to in the future. If they survived this night. But being with his mate just now only reinforced how much was on the line. He would do all in his power to keep them both alive so that they could make love for many years to come, growing old together, holding each other's hearts into eternity.

And when had he become a damn poet, Jake wondered? He almost had to laugh at himself. Ria had changed him in fundamental ways, but he liked it. He liked being with her and what it had done to him. He liked the man he was when he was with her. And he loved her more than life itself.

He would move heaven and earth to keep her safe. And he had seen what was in store. The real test would come later tonight.

The cabin had become a war room, more or less, in the time they'd been gone, Ria discovered. There were maps of the area up on one wall and more than just her Royal Guard gathered around, discussing coverage. There were a lot of foxes in the room, by the scent of things. At least a half dozen of them were briefing her people on the terrain and being briefed in return on what to expect from the newcomers in their territory.

All in all, Ria was impressed by the way the different kinds of shifters were working together. *Pantera noir* usually lived somewhat apart from all other shifters because of their rarity and the danger their queen always seemed to be in. Before Ria's mother was killed by their enemies, she had been hunted. It was her mother who had started the tradition of the Nyx being almost constantly on the move.

In the old days, access to the Nyx had been open to all shifters who wanted to breach the veil and talk to their departed. It was the Nyx's sacred duty to be the intermediary, helping those still in this mortal realm by delivering the wisdom of those who had passed on to the next.

The Nyxs of old had made their homes in different places around the world, usually setting it up so that other shifters could reach them for open sessions during the three nights each month surrounding the new moon. Many pilgrimages had been made to wherever the Nyx chose to hold court over the centuries. It was only in recent years that she'd had to take to the road and hide her presence as much as possible.

Those who needed to find her could, of course. There was a screening system that would line up those who sought an audience during the new moon ceremony. Modern shifters would call a number, leave their information and if they checked out with a specially tasked Guard contingent, they would be given a time and place to be, if the Nyx was nearby. And in very special cases, she would make surprise visits to those who couldn't come to her.

But if they didn't prevail tonight, there would be no more traveling. No more mediating between this world and the next. No more Nyx.

They had to prevent that. And so all these good people were gathered in this cabin, ready to go to war for her and the burden she carried.

"You all have your assignments." Jake's voice carried to her over the murmurs of the gathered shifters.

He'd left her side when they arrived and checked in with Geir. Jake motioned to her to join him now, at the center of the group. The warriors made a path for her to join Jake and Geir at their center.

She knew her role now. She had to say something. Something inspirational that would inspire everyone. Too bad she had no idea what to say. Thanks were paltry, but all she really had. She didn't want any more people to die on her behalf. She didn't even want them to get hurt, but she knew what would happen tonight. They would get hurt and some might die.

Who was she kidding? *All* of them would die if the *Venifucus* succeeded. No way would Elspeth leave anybody that served the Light alive if she came through the veil. Everyone here would be the first to die. The first of many. Too many to think about.

She took her place at Jake's side and felt the warmth of his support, which meant more than she could say. Geir too, supported her, in his way. And then she realized that everyone here was supporting her in their own way—even the foxes she had only just met. And then she knew what she had to say. She had to speak to them from her heart.

"I can't thank you all enough for staying and being willing to face what will come with courage and brave hearts. The *Venifucus* have been chasing me for a long time and I'm sorry I brought this trouble to your Pack." She nodded toward the fox Alpha. She hadn't seen him before because he was standing near the center of the circle, surrounded by his people. "The sad truth is, if the enemy succeeds in their plans, there will be no safe place for anyone who serves the Light. The last time Elspeth walked this earth, many lives were lost in the battle to contain her. If the *Venifucus* succeed in bringing her back, which they have attempted several times recently, the pattern will repeat and the war will begin anew."

She paused to look into each pair of eyes, making sure she looked at every single person gathered to support her. It was important that they knew they weren't just faceless, nameless soldiers to her. They were people. Amazing people who were willing to stand up for what was right.

"We can't let that happen," she stated simply. To her surprise, an edge of steel had entered her voice and even more shocking was the answering chorus of agreement that came from the gathered warriors.

"We'll send them straight back to hell, where they belong," Geir shouted, raising one clenched fist above his head. He shook his fist and a cheer went up along with every other male's fist, shaking their promise toward the heavens.

Ria watched them, realizing that this group, which consisted of three or more separate groups had united for a common cause. They were behind her, but more importantly, they were against the enemy. The foxes appeared to not only accept, but welcome the interloping *pantera* and Others in their territory.

Likewise, the different groups of Guards seemed to be meshing well with everyone—though Ria had expected they would work well together, even though they were usually on different shifts. They'd all been trained by Geir and those like him. They worked together, even if they didn't usually work at the same time. And Geir seemed to have taken a position of leadership over all, as it should be. He was, by far, the most experienced warrior they had.

They were a united force, but would it be enough? Ria sent up a little prayer to the Goddess, hoping for the best.

This time, when Ria left the cabin, she was surrounded by her people. Guards she had known and worked with for years escorted her directly to the stone circle. They still had some time to prepare, according to Jake's vision, but they were taking no chances. Everyone was getting in their planned positions with plenty of time to spare.

Jake was going over last minute plans with Geir as they walked. She wanted to walk with him, but she knew her Guard was nervous enough as it was without her misbehaving. She kept throwing glances back over her shoulder, catching glimpses of Jake's strong profile as he walked along.

He'd availed himself of the fox's armory. A giant, dark rifle of some kind was slung across his back. Two side arms were strapped to his thighs and there were other weapons tucked here and there around his person. He was armed to the teeth, as it were, and looked very comfortable with the shocking amount of gear.

When they arrived at the stone circle, her people dispersed, but didn't go far. The Royal Guard was to remain inside the circle with her, though as out of sight as they could manage. A few shifted shape, hiding in the darkness, their black pelts blending in with the night shadows.

Ria had brought a few props with her. A shiny, shallow metal bowl and a bottle of water were the main accoutrements she would need. She placed the bowl on the altar stone, blushing at her recent memories of this particular setting. She poured out the water into the bowl and let it settle, placing a few other items nearby as if she needed them for some arcane ceremony.

In truth, all she needed was the amulet that rested around her neck and her own energy to open the portal, but hopefully the enemy didn't know that. They seemed to know an awful lot though. And if the intel they had was correct, at least one among them knew one heck of a lot more than he should.

"Are you all set here?" Jake's voice came to her from above and she looked up to find him nearby. She straightened from her bent position and went over to him.

She walked straight into his arms. It felt so good when his strong arms closed around her. He made her feel safe. He made her feel invincible.

"Are you okay?" He asked in a soft, almost uncertain voice. She looked up at him, meeting his gaze.

"Just a little anxious, I guess," she admitted.

"It's okay to be scared," he offered, his gaze concerned. "Just don't let it freeze you up. But I don't have to tell you. You know how to use the adrenaline to your advantage. I've seen you do it. You're strong, Ria. The strongest person I've ever known."

When he said it in that tender tone, she almost believed him. It was good of him to give her a pep talk. She really needed it about now. The stakes had never been so dire. But then again, she'd never had this much help before.

All she knew was that she wanted to stop running. She wanted to take a stand and have this out once and for all with the evil one who had somehow learned her secret. She wanted the *Venifucus* to know that she would not be easy prey. She had teeth of her own and many allies who would fight on her side against them.

"Thanks, Jake." She reached up and stroked his hair, running her fingers through the short strands. "You're one in a million, you know that?" She smiled and tugged his head downward, wanting one last kiss before they faced danger together.

He obliged, lowering his head so their lips met in a tender conflagration that spoke of desire, but also of the deep and abiding love they had discovered within their hearts for each other. Her cat wanted to rub up against him reveled in the way he held her. Her human heart ached, wanting this uncertainty over so they could lock themselves away for a honeymoon neither of them would ever forget.

Soon. Everything would be decided soon.

One way or the other.

Everything was in place. Willard Fontanbleau surveyed the preparations of his small army with a gloating sort of glee. The Nyx wouldn't escape this time. Those who sought to protect her wouldn't even know what hit them. Between the ground troops—mere cannon fodder as far as Willard was concerned—and the little surprise he had learned from the leviathan, the enemy shifters who peppered the mountain approach to the sacred site on Mount Sterling Ridge, wouldn't stand a chance.

Willard would only enter the area when a sufficient path had been cleared by the mercenaries he had hired or coerced into working for him. He was certain there were a number of agents among his troopers, spying on his actions for his enemies on the Council, but Willard didn't mind. He was very much in favor of the philosophy that said *keep your friends close and your enemies closer.*

He kept an elite squad of paid mercenaries—men he had interviewed himself—to be his personal guard. Only after the others had cleared a path, would Willard arrive to confront the Nyx himself. He was the only one who could do it. He was the only one who knew her secret.

The one and only time Willard had ever successfully connected with a soul on the other side of the veil, he had learned the secret of the Nyx. He still wasn't entirely certain the soul he had communed with had intended to divulge the secret, but it had come out nonetheless. In the ancient one's worry for the current generation, it had connected with him and communicated more than it should have—or possibly would have—if not for his quick thinking and the spells he had thrown at the being once the first images started to come through to Willard.

He had not heard words. Not the way the Nyx was purported to do. No, he had seen images. He saw an amulet. The being that had connected with him was very worried about the amulet. It took a while before Willard was able to figure out why and exactly who he had connected with that long ago night when magic had been flying thick and heavy on the ground.

It had taken a lot of time to track down the various historical accounts of the Nyx and her powers that had finally convinced him of what he had learned. Nowhere was it written or recorded that the Nyx had any sort of physical object that brought her the power she wielded, but when Willard finally figured out who he had connected with, he realized he could not doubt the source of the image or the powers associated with the amulet he saw.

For he had been in communion with one of the ancient Nyx. Perhaps the first one, herself. He couldn't be certain which Nyx, exactly. But one of the oldest ones. One of the most powerful—even across the veil. She had eventually broken his spells that tied her to him and allowed him to rummage through her memories. He'd seen a great deal in that short time, however. Enough to send him on the quest of his life. The quest to kill the Nyx and steal her amulet—the source of her power—for his own.

Things were falling into place and the final confrontation would come soon. Willard was in the lower staging area, out of sight of the defenders' first string of sentries. His military commander had sent out scouts and they had even taken the initiative to capture one of the enemy shifters for interrogation. What they had learned gave Willard pause.

The Nyx had taken a mate. And the new mate was the one who had orchestrated her escape from the last attempt on her life. Apparently this mate had military training and was a force to be reckoned with. Willard didn't like the sound of that, but he also saw a possible opportunity to exploit.

According to the prisoner, the Nyx's new mate was human. Willard almost laughed when he heard that part. A woman of such power mating a weak human. Regardless of the man's military skill, he was still just human. Easily defeated. Humans were only good for slave labor in Willard's view and they would soon relearn their place when Elspeth came back to power.

For now, it was a simple matter to send out new orders to every man in his small army. Any human found on the mountain was to be captured alive. They could kill all the shifters they wanted—and Willard hoped that number was high—but the humans were to be spared and examined. And when Willard identified the one he wanted, he would use the Nyx's new mate to bring her to her knees before him.

The order went out and the time came for their assault on the mountain ridge. Willard had timed it so that he should have the Nyx and her all-important amulet, by the time the new moon was at its peak. He would waste no time, using the blood of his enemies and his dying soldiers alike to fuel the spells he would need to bring Elspeth back this very night, if at all possible. At the very least, he would make his first attempt tonight, as soon as possible. The amulet only worked on the new moon, so it would be a month before he could try again if he failed to open the doorway this night. He had to try.

For now though, as he sent his first troops up the mountain, Willard prepared a little magical surprise for the fighters up there on the ridge. He gathered his power and launched a spell directed at the water he could feel flowing up there—a small lake from what he could sense, and a stream that would work very well for his purposes.

And his main purpose this night was terror...and diversion.

CHAPTER ELEVEN

When the enemy arrived it wasn't with fanfare. No, they slithered in, past the outer perimeter, taking some of the foxes down as they went. The rest of the line did their duty, communicating what they could before their positions were overrun, doing their best to herd the enemy into the defenses they had constructed over the past few hours.

Jake did his best to keep up with developments. The battlefield was spread out all over the mountain, but it appeared their plan to direct the flow of enemy forces in one particular pathway was working, for the most part. They'd set up several traps which were being sprung on unwary *Venifucus* foot soldiers.

From initial reports, some were mercenaries. Some were low-level mages with minimal power but a whole lot of attitude and some were humans who had a serious grudge against anything with fur. The human hunters—for that's what they looked like, geared up like Elmer Fudd in plaid and holding rifles—weren't really prepared for the onslaught. Many went down under pressure from the defenders and didn't get back up.

Jake started to feel a little optimistic when he heard splashing from the small lake just south of the stone circle. It wasn't a good sort of splashing. Jake moved through the trees, only to find Tom Kinkaid down on one knee, bleeding profusely as the biggest, sharpest-toothed river monster he'd ever seen sank his teeth in one more time before Tom got the upper hand and flung it against the rocks.

But there were more of them. Even now, Jake could see the waters around the shoreline where Tom stood, bubbling with an evil red glow that was caused by nothing natural. There was magic at work here. Bad magic, if Jake was any judge. He ran to the shoreline and took Tom's arm, hauling him backward.

"Let's get you out of reach of those teeth, buddy." Tom didn't resist, but helped as best he could while bleeding all over the rocky soil. Geir showed up at that moment and took charge of Tom.

Jake didn't waste time. He took aim at the toothy head that popped above the water and fired. As the creature went down, a melee seemed to happen just beneath the surface. The other monster fish were ripping apart the one Jake had shot. He hefted a shotgun the foxes had been nice enough to lend him and started firing into the turbulent waters, unable to really see what he accomplished, though after a few well-placed shots, the activity beneath the dark water seemed to abate somewhat.

He went back to check on Tom. Geir had applied bandages and seemed to have the bleeding slowed, but the selkie was down for the count. His pale skin shone in the darkness as he grabbed Jake's arm.

"Warn Jacki! Those things are headed her way. Oh, Goddess!" His head fell back as pain seemed to overtake him for a moment. Whether it was just physical pain or the pain of worry for his sister, Jake didn't know. Probably both.

"On it." Jake paused to pass the warning over his radio. "Can you still shoot? This area is about to be overrun. Can you handle yourself on land? There's no way you're getting back in the water with those things in there."

"I could use that shotgun if you can spare it," Tom said, eyeing the long barrel. Jake handed it over without a word.

He detached the pouch that held the shells and gave that to Tom also.

"I'll make sure he's hidden," Geir said, though his face was pained. Jake got the impression the tiger-shifter wanted to run to Jacki's aid, but couldn't leave Tom to die. And they both knew Jake had to stay mobile.

He was coordinating things because he was the only one who knew what he'd seen in his vision. Any little thing might give them the edge they needed, but Jake wouldn't recognize it until he saw it unfold. Only then could he act on the warnings of the vision, though he'd made various preparations for the things he could.

Jake grasped Tom's shoulder, pausing only a moment before he left on the double to help the selkie girl, if he could. If those fish-monster things had taken Tom down, he didn't have much hope his little sister would fare any better.

Jake followed the line of the stream that flowed northward and around the bottom of the stone circle. Jacki was stationed there, at the point where the stream meandered closest to the circle.

Jake saw Beau first. The angry tiger-shifter had his teeth bared as he used his own shotgun to stave off large numbers of the monsters from the woman who stood in the middle of the stream, her arms raised. She was chanting and whatever she was doing was turning the monsters back into small, harmless fish again—but not fast enough.

Beau was killing all he could, but the monster-fish kept coming. Eventually, there would be too many and then the selkie woman would go down, like her brother had.

And then Jake saw some of the creatures slither out of the stream and head over land toward the stone circle. Apparently there'd been some amphibians and snakes in the lake that had been changed as well. And one spiky armored thing that must've been a turtle.

Gunfire was heard all up and down the mountain now as Jake called for reinforcements. Ben and the Rojas brothers showed up with shotguns and even machetes to hack at the slithering things from the other side of the stream. It felt like as soon as they killed one, two more would take its place and they were getting closer and closer to where the selkie woman was standing in the middle of the stream, her arms upraised as she chanted.

Jake didn't recognize the words or even the language that she spoke, but he felt the power. It was rising like a tide. Something big was coming and she was at the center of it. Her arms reached for the sky and her palms turned toward the oncoming rush of deformed creatures with massive teeth.

Jake kept firing and doing his best to stop any amphibian-type creatures that tried to move onto the land. These things were like something out of a horror movie and they just kept coming. Whatever Jacki Kinkaid was up to, she'd better do it soon because those things were almost to her. If she didn't release all that power she was building up real soon, it would all be for naught.

And then she did.

She clapped her hands above her head and it was as if lighting had struck the earth and especially the water. Arcing light bolted out from her hands to the creatures in the water only a foot from her, morphing them back into their original forms. Hideous fanged serpents became small harmless tadpoles. River monsters became small fish with no teeth at all and sweet dispositions.

The lightning-like flash swept from creature to creature down the stream and all the way back to the lake, changing everything in its path back to what it had been. Mostly harmless. A snapping turtle lost the spiky armor and pincers and became merely a six-inch long turtle again, snapping at the stick that blocked its path rather than Ari Rojas's leg, which it had been aiming for before it was changed.

Jake saw Ari reach down and pick up the little creature, placing it gently back on the bank, near the water. With a little shove, the turtle headed back downstream, toward the lake that was its home. The silence in the aftermath of the thunderclap of magical energy was startling, but all too soon, bullets started flying again.

The river monster attack had done its job—distracting Jake from the real ground assault that had made major progress up the mountain while they had been busy fighting off mutant fish. He took one last look around the area. Jacki Kinkaid was down, but the two tigers were protecting her body on the far bank. They'd hidden her in a small thicket of bushes near the bank and one furry tiger was lying in wait near her unconscious body, the other—Beau Champlain— was prowling nearby on two legs, holding an assault rifle. Jacki was about as well-protected as she was going to get on this mountain tonight. She had done an amazing thing in reversing the spell on the lake creatures. She had earned a moment's rest while she recovered from her magical efforts.

Jake hoped that's all it was as he turned away to rejoin the battle. He liked Jacki and admired the magic and courage she had just displayed. He'd hate to think it had killed her to help them.

Jake checked in with the different groups only to find that the foxes' position had been overrun. The enemy ground troops were now within the outer perimeter. Those who remained of the fox scouts were making their way to a rally point to regroup. Some were helping get their injured to safety.

Jake stumbled upon a group of injured and helped get them to the only place that was still safe up here—the stone circle. He saw Ria, still protected within the circle for the moment, but they didn't have time to talk. He merely handed off the injured and made his way back to the battle, vowing again silently to do all he could to keep the enemy from getting close to her. If they could pick off the ground troops below, maybe they could head off the more desperate parts of his vision.

Then again, after all these years, he knew how his visions worked. Most of the time, even if he did all he could to prevent a bad event from occurring, it still happened. And he had seen some pretty bad things in his most recent vision.

Things he couldn't bring himself to tell Ria. Things that would only worry her needlessly.

If any of those things occurred, he would deal with them. He had prepared as best he could for all the contingencies he had seen, and now only time would tell how it would all work out. He had been forewarned. He hoped he was for-armed enough to deal with it.

Jacki Kinkaid was groggy, but still awake. She had been able to stumble to the far side of the stream with Beau's help. He had helped her hide in a little nest of bushes, her back against a tree. She had wanted him to stay near, but he had insisted on standing guard outside of her hiding place.

When a shifter in tiger form slunk through an opening in the bushes to join her, at first her heart skipped a beat, thinking Beau had come to her. But it wasn't Beau. It was the strange tiger. Geir. The sensei. The scary one.

Only he didn't look quite so scary in his fur. In fact, he looked...majestic. Protective. Sort of amazing. She reached out and he allowed her to stroke her fingers through the fur near his neck.

"Have you come to keep me company?" she asked rhetorically, knowing he couldn't answer in words. She was well acquainted with the limitations of wearing your fur.

He shifted shape quickly and crouched before her, naked as the day he was born. Shifters were used to nakedness, since almost all had to disrobe before they could become their animal—or else spend a lot of money replacing their wardrobe all the time. Why then was she so affected by Master Geir's nudity? She found herself looking away, casting shy glances his way and fighting the heat that wanted to stain her cheeks.

Then she remembered. Geir had been with her brother. Shyness was forgotten.

"Where is Tom?" she demanded in a fearful whisper.

"He's hurt, but still alive. He asked me to check on you before we attempted to regroup. I left him with a very brave circle of snapping turtles around him. They were trying to protect him," Geir shook his head with a rueful smile. "Darndest thing I've ever seen."

"Creatures of the water like us. We protect them when we can," Jacki replied softly.

"As you say. I'll get your brother and bring him to you. It is too dangerous for you to try to get to him. The woods are filling fast with enemies. Stay hidden and allow Beau to do his job. I'll be back shortly with your brother."

Geir shifted quickly into his tiger shape, pausing briefly in the battle form that was half-human and half-tiger. He was a fearsome creature no matter what his form, she realized as he slunk silently off into the dark woods.

She pretty much held her breath until he was back. She was afraid for him. For Tom. And for Beau. She didn't want any of the men she felt responsible for in this situation getting hurt. It didn't matter that they were all highly trained warriors. She felt responsible. It was part of her calling, she supposed.

She thought about ways to keep them all safe in the moments to come. The gunfire was getting closer and she heard things moving not too far away from her hiding spot. The battle would be upon them all soon and she was the next best thing to a burden, now that her task in this battle had been carried out.

She had to think of a way to do one thing more—to keep them safe. If she had the energy left to do anything at all.

Geir slunk into her circle of bushes on two feet, with Tom on his back in a fireman's hold. Jacki tried not to gasp as she saw the many gashes and cuts on her brother's body. He was still clothed and many of the ragged bits of his clothing were stained deep red with his blood. He was unconscious when Geir lay him gently at Jacki's side.

"I'll stay with you for a few moments more, but then I must go help my students and the queen," Geir reported, crouching on Tom's other side, helping to lift his legs and put a pile of fallen branches and leaves beneath them.

He also took off Tom's gear belt and dug within some of the pouches, extracting medical supplies which Jacki and Geir both put to good use, staunching the flow of blood and holding together the worst of the deep wounds with field sutures and butterfly bandages.

Jacki had heard a lot about Master Geir, but she didn't really know him. It surprised her that he had come to help her, but she guessed she shouldn't have been too shocked. The man was the best of the best. He was the one who trained Royal Guards for the *pantera noir* queen.

He had volunteered to look out for the selkies and their task. He would see that through. He was a protector through and through. A true Alpha male.

And here she was, a damsel in distress. That magical thunderclap had taken almost all she had, but she'd been smart. She had kept a tiny bit of reserve so she wouldn't be completely unconscious and vulnerable after the fact. She still felt like a wet dishrag though, and she needed more than a few minutes to rest. But there was no time. Things were moving fast on the dark mountain. Tom needed her help and any minute now there would be more enemy than friend on this side of the stone circle.

She felt okay about her part in the night's action though. She had done what only she could to end the threat from the water. That was why she'd been sent here, after all. Tom might think that he was supposed to have done it, and he might be really angry that she'd been in danger when he woke up, but Tante Sophia had been very specific in her instructions. She had also advised Jacki not to mention all the details to Tom. The women in her family knew how to stick together.

A tiny smile lifted the corners of her mouth for a moment, but her smile faded in the next instant as the sounds of battle erupted very close to her hiding place. Geir dropped the bandage he'd been working with and shifted his weight as if preparing to leave. He was readiness itself when the sound of gunfire came from almost directly above them. She looked up only to realize that Beau had climbed the tree she leaned against, perching above in a sort of improvised sniper's nest.

He was picking off enemies while they were still some distance from the tree, but he seemed to be firing faster and faster, as more and more enemies came into his sights. She worried for his safety. It wouldn't be long before they figured out where those deadly shots were coming from. It was almost time for her to commit her final act this night. Something the men wouldn't be happy about, but something she was determined to do.

And then Beau tumbled from the tree, bleeding heavily from a leg wound. Jacki watched in horror as he thudded to the ground, just outside her circle of bushes. She tried to move forward, but Geir blocked her path.

"He needs help," she tried to reason with the sensei.

"I'll get him. You stay here and keep your head down," Geir promised, his mouth a grim line as he moved silently through the bushes, leaving her once again.

Jacki worried for Geir almost as much as she worried for Beau. She had known Beau for a while now, and she had admired him from afar for all that time. He had kept his distance until this trip and while his demeanor had been grumpy at best, she thought his bad temper might be because he cared. At least a little. For whatever reason, he was keeping himself aloof, but the more she was around him, the more she thought maybe there was something special about the big, angry cat.

She had sworn to herself that when this was over, she was going to confront him to see what he would do. She would either fight with him, or jump his bones. It could go either way, but no matter what happened, it would relieve the incredible tension between them. Only, if he died here tonight, she would never get the chance to discover what he might have been to her. She might lose him before she'd ever discovered what fate had in store for them.

And Master Geir. What was it about him that made her—an experienced selkie magic user—blush? It shouldn't be possible, but all Geir had to do was shift in front of her and she felt an almost overwhelming feeling of femininity overcome her. It was an incredibly odd feeling for her and one that made her stop to question why she was so attracted and affected by two powerful men? Were they both special? Or was one somehow interfering with her perception of the other? Was one of them her mate? Or—even more shocking—were they both?

She only knew she couldn't let either one of them die without finding the answer to her questions. Geir was still unharmed, but it felt like it was only a matter of time before he'd be out there, in the middle of everything. She didn't know him well, but she knew he was a man of action. So was Tom. So was Beau, for that matter. None of them would want to be sidelined, but two of her three men were not in control of their fates at the moment. Geir was in danger as well and it hurt her heart to think of him going into battle without her or Beau or even Tom to back him up. He could be hurt! He could be killed.

Jacki vowed with the very last of her strength, she would not let that happen. She brought her hands together, rubbing the palms in a circular motion she used to help draw her personal magic forth. Geir wasn't going to like what she had planned, but she had set the spell in motion and it would be too late to stop her by the time he realized what she had done.

Geir came into the circle of bushes for the second time, carrying an injured man. He put Beau down on the other side of her, already tearing at the cloth of his pants that covered the profusely bleeding leg wound. It was obvious Geir knew first aid. He would be there to help the other two when she completed her spell.

"Where's my gun?" Beau croaked out. He was still somewhat conscious though she doubted that would last long.

Geir reached for something behind him and then dropped a huge sniper rifle near Beau's hand. Beau took possession of the giant gun with clear relief.

"Thanks." Beau checked over the rifle while Geir saw to his wound. Neither of them paid any attention to Jacki as she began forming her spell. This would take whatever reserves she had left, but it would be worth it to keep them all safe.

Finally, as the magic was set to release and a static charge built up inside the circle, Geir looked up from his work on Beau's leg. Beau was looking at her too, and neither man looked happy.

"What are you doing?" Geir demanded. He tried to stand but the electric tingle of magic wouldn't let him move. Not until the spell had been cast. It was a powerful one and it held him in place.

"I'm going to raise a shield. It'll be a bubble of protection around this spot," she told them.

"You can't," Geir protested, as she expected. "My duty is out there. I need to protect the Nyx."

"No." Jacki felt a tear trickle down her cheek, but ignored it. "I won't let you get hurt too. You're mine to protect tonight and I'm going to do it. I know you're not happy, but I know this is the right thing to do." She gathered her power for the final ramp up before releasing the spell. She had to make this good or Geir would break it. She couldn't let that happen. She had to protect him. "Forgive me, Master Geir, and trust me that this is the right thing to do. I feel it in my bones. In my heart and in my soul."

Geir looked taken aback by her statement, but she didn't stop to ponder his reaction. She let loose the spell and felt the power spin out from her in a vortex of protection. She let go of all the power she had been drawing to her. Power from the earth. Power from the nearby water. Power from within her very soul. All of it she dispersed into a dome shape, following the circle of the bushes and tree, using their living, green energy as well.

She saw the flare of the dome for a moment or two before she felt the magic pour out of her into it. Powering it. Keeping it strong against the enemy and hidden from evil.

The foot soldiers would pass right by it, never knowing it—or they—were hidden within. Only an enemy mage might be able to sense its presence, but by tying it to the earth, the water, and the growing things all around them, she had made it the next best thing to impenetrable.

For now, it would do. And she had her aunt's foretelling that she and the tigers would survive this. Jacki collapsed as the power drained out of her, only dimly aware of the arms that reached out to catch her and ease her trip to the earth. She looked up into icy blue eyes. Geir.

"What have you done?" Geir asked, able to move now that the power had landed where it she had intended.

She had very little strength left, but she had to try to make him understand.

"I did what I was sent here to do—as have you. So my Tante Sophia said. She foresaw all of this."

"Did she see how it was going to end?" Beau asked.

"No. But she did say that if I used all my skill and strength, myself and two tigers would survive to fight another day. Since you two are the only two tigers here…" She left off speaking, her energy failing rapidly. "Geir, look after Beau and my brother. I'll be okay after I sleep. Don't worry."

He held her close to his chest and the look in his baby blues nearly melted her heart. She read anger, as she had expected, but also concern, care and something that looked a lot like…love?

That was the last thing she remembered for several hours, and it was a pleasant, if perplexing memory to take with her into unconsciousness.

The Golden Jackal observed all on the field of battle. He had taken a sniper position up high in one of the many trees in this thick forest. It was one that afforded him a better view of the battlefield than perhaps, anyone else. He saw the selkie priestess—for surely with that kind of power, Jacki Kinkaid had to be a servant of the Lady—rid the waters of the evil spell that had turned simple water creatures into the stuff of nightmares. He had seen the tiger-shifter sniper fall from his perch and had obliged by taking out the enemy soldier who had shot Beau in the leg.

Seth had provided cover fire, though nobody on the ground was truly aware of his position. But that was okay. The jackal preferred to work in the shadows. He didn't need recognition or accolades. He had his reward in a job well done—and an enemy slaughtered.

But there were too many of them. As soon as he and the other snipers shot one down, there were two more to take his place. Something was driving the foot soldiers. Something relentless. Something that didn't care about sending its men to die. Something evil.

Seth watched it all and did what he could to stem the tide. He helped his new allies on the ground where he could. He kept an eye on the rest of his small squad—Ben and the two Rojas brothers. They were all acting as snipers, since they had particular skill with long range weapons. And Ben was human. He might be a hell of a soldier, but he couldn't shapeshift, which was a distinct disadvantage in this battle.

Even as Seth thought this, he saw what remained of the fox Pack converge on several attackers, taking them down neat and clean. He hadn't thought foxes could be quite so vicious, but they were protecting their home as well as the fabled *pantera noir* queen.

She might not be the same species, but the Nyx held a special place among shifters of all kinds. Her sacrifice, it was said, allowed for a sacred communication with those on the other side of the veil. Her abilities were Goddess-blessed and Goddess-endowed. All those who followed the Mother of All were bound to help the Nyx as she helped them talk with those who had been taken to the other side too soon, or with words left unspoken.

It was every good shifter's honor to help protect the Nyx. Even Seth had to admit to a feeling of sentimentality when it came to Ria. It didn't hurt that she looked like everyone's little sister either. Her appearance inspired an impulse in most shifters who had any protective instincts at all, to help her, protect her, and keep her safe.

That wasn't a bad attribute for a monarch who had lived most of her life on the run. Perhaps it was something she cultivated, Seth mused, even as he picked off another enemy soldier. These woods would need one hell of a cleansing after this battle. All right under the humans' noses. Thank goodness they were far enough out in the country—and up on the mountain ridge—that no nosy humans might get caught up in the middle of all of this. Seth suspected magic at work, to hide the sounds of battle, regardless.

Seth could see part of the stone circle from his vantage point. He noted with approval the fact that the injured were being brought there—the most heavily defended point on the ridge. They would make their final stand there, and while it might not be the safest place in the world, it was the safest place for anyone who had been fighting this battle. For without doubt, the enemy would murder everyone not on their side if they managed to win the day.

Seth was dead set against that outcome. He might be a mercenary, but when it came to good versus evil, he was pretty firmly on the good side, though others might not always see it that way. Still, whatever Seth had done in the past, he had always worked on the side of Light—even if he was playing the long game and not interested in immediate outcomes. Some might say he was arguing semantics, but Seth had contemplated his positions each time he'd sold his skills to a high bidder. He had never accepted any job that would cross over his personal boundaries, and never would.

It was high time the jackal threw in his lot officially with the good guys. Which was why he was here on this mountain ridge. He had declared himself on the right side of this battle—much to the surprise of many in the covert community. He'd lost a bit of his mystery, but that couldn't be helped. No longer could he tread the fine line between good and evil. The day for reckoning was too close now. It was time to come out of the shadows...at least a little. Even if it went against his longstanding habits.

Seth approved of the way the Royal Guard—some of the best fighters he'd ever seen, and that was saying a lot—formed a circle of protection within the standing stones, around their queen and the wounded. Ria stood ready, but seemed to be doing something near the altar stone, just out of Seth's line of sight. He could feel magic gathering though—whether it was good or bad, he wasn't quite sure, but it was massive, whatever it was.

And then he saw the last of the outer perimeter positions get overrun. The enemy was within the outer defenses and everyone was regrouping. The selkie priestess had done something in the small thicket of bushes in which she and the two tigers hid. Seth couldn't see them now, which meant the woman had raised some kind of protective shield. Smart move, since Beau wasn't going anywhere and the priestess was probably running on her last dregs of energy if she had any left after that final protective spell. Master Geir would watch over both of them, Seth knew, though it was unexpected.

Seth had thought nothing could tear the tiger away from defense of the Nyx, but then Seth had noticed the way Geir watched Jacki Kinkaid. It was subtle, but there was definitely something there. After witnessing that, it didn't surprise Seth too much to see where Geir had decided to make his stand. The Nyx was precious, but so was the priestess. Both needed protection and Jacki had only a wounded man to look after her while Ria had every soldier on the mountain on their side and her elite Royal Guard watching her back, not to mention her mate. The seer.

Powerful allies indeed. Seth couldn't fault Master Geir for taking the initiative and watching over the selkie priestess. He might've done the same.

The tide was turning and not in the defenders' favor. Seth could do little more than pick off those he could see but there were too many for one man. Too many for the team of four that had distributed their skills around the stone circle. Seth was placed in the southeast sniper location. Ben had southwest, while Ari and Pax were northwest and northeast respectively. They had split up the perimeter of the stone circle to lie in wait.

Of the four, Seth was seeing the most action, though all of them were kept busy picking off intruders. Still, Seth had the best vantage point since the main attack force seemed to be coming from his direction. Jacki Kinkaid and the tigers had hidden just a little south of his position and Seth assumed the Royal Guard would be manning the cardinal points of north, south, east and west from within the circle of stones.

Jake though, was a wild card. He'd been traipsing up and down the mountain, helping here and there, going between groups, spreading news and helping where he could. Seth hadn't seen the sense in it. What could a lone human do ferrying information between groups of shapeshifters? Seth hadn't expected much, but he'd been surprised by the effect the seer's words had on the groups he spoke to throughout the running battle.

Jake had shown courage and stamina as well as skill Seth hadn't expected. The human had taken down opponents without hesitation and helped get the injured to safety within the stone circle. But he didn't stay there. Surprisingly, rather than stay with his mate, Jake kept making forays out from the circle. It was as if he was looking for something, Seth realized.

And then Seth watched, helpless, and with a sinking feeling in his gut, as something found Jake instead.

CHAPTER TWELVE

Jake knew the moment he pushed his luck just a little too far. Or maybe just far enough. He felt the cold barrel of a gun against his neck as a harsh voice ordered him to put his hands up. Jake complied, knowing with a little sinking feeling in his stomach that at least one of the really bad things he'd foreseen was about to come true.

He didn't struggle as the enemy soldiers pushed him around. He didn't fight back. He knew if he did, he would die. Simple as that. The vision had shown him the consequences of fighting—and what might happen if he chose to control his instincts and not fight back...yet. Jake had decided to go with the latter option. There was still a slim chance of pulling this out and he had to take it.

"What the hell is a human doing up here among the animals?" Jake's captor sneered.

Jake didn't reply. He had to keep his cool or this could turn out very badly. It bothered him to stay silent, but he knew in this instance it was very necessary to his possible survival.

"Cat got yer tongue?" the man asked while securing Jake's hands behind his back with zip ties. He then prodded Jake once more with the gun, now bumping hard into his kidney. The man laughed when Jake continued to ignore his taunts.

"It's your lucky day, buddy. The big kahuna wanted any human we found on this mountain alive for some reason. Let's go. He has to see you before he decides if I get to kill you or not."

Another hard poke to the kidney got Jake moving. It pained him to realize they were moving up the mountain, toward the stone circle. Could the enemy have gotten so far in such a short time? It was possible. One of the scenarios he'd foreseen had him meeting the face of evil inside the stone circle. If this was that particular possible future, Jake had a good idea what to do. He set to work, thinking about how to best utilize the tools he had pre-positioned based on the multiple scenarios he had foreseen.

When evil walked into the circle of standing stones, Ria felt it immediately. The portal had opened moments before, swirling in a light show she had seldom seen before, a viscous green circle positioned in thin air, right above the altar stone. Ria knew the energy of the standing stones was amplifying the power of the amulet. It was a phenomenon she had only seen a couple of times before.

Ria was not in control of this manifestation. The energies of the amulet and the stones had called to each other and the portal had opened. Ria could hear the wailing on the other side as the terminating point of the portal was pulled and stretched from the next realm toward something...else.

Evil was inside the circle and trying to influence where the portal led. Ria did what little she could to block it. Her personal energy was great, but she wasn't sure it would be enough to stop the depth of depravity she now felt inside the sacred place.

And then she felt the help pouring through from the other side. All those who had gone before were there, at the terminus, using all their energy to keep the portal in their realm. There were some amazing beings in that other realm, but they too, it seemed, were under attack somehow. She didn't know how it all worked on the other side. There were many, many things she was not allowed to know—or even to ask. What came after death in the mortal realm was supposed to be a mystery and there were rules each Nyx had followed, handed down by the Goddess Herself, it was said.

But Ria could hear the skirmishing in the background, beyond the veil, as if from a distant room. She also heard the voices of those who were defending the portal on the far side, offering advice that only she could hear. Ria followed the words of those she knew and trusted, holding strong against the invading power. Among them were priestesses and mages of antiquity who had come to share their wisdom and knowledge with Ria. They told her things she had never even guessed at before, teaching her ways to defend the portal from magical attacks.

She could do this all day, she thought, having absorbed the secret knowledge from those who had passed. She took a moment to look around the stone circle. Her Royal Guard blocked most of her view, having formed a circle of protection around her, the injured, and the altar, but she could see a bit as they moved and fought. Even the injured who could still hold a gun were helping defend the portal.

Ria's gaze went from face to face among the enemy, looking for the one that was trying to commandeer the portal for his own use. She could sense it was male energy, but that didn't help much. It looked like there were a vast majority of males arrayed against her people. That might mean something, but Ria had no idea what. If they survived this, it was something she'd have to look into, but for now, it was important that they hold strong against the enemy, even though the situation looked grave.

Her advisors on the other side of the portal cheered her on, giving her hope. They stood firm with her, helping her in whatever way they could, even as it seemed they fought on their side of the veil as well. They didn't seem as overwhelmed over there as they were here, but she couldn't be truly sure of anything just now.

And then Jake stumbled into the stone circle and Ria's

heart stopped. At first, she didn't know what she was seeing. Jake was in the center of a group of enemy fighters and they were walking toward the eastern side of the circle. Was he with them willingly?

Her heart skipped a beat, then resumed as she noted the way his hands were pulled back and tied together behind him. His head was down, but she knew he wasn't there of his own volition. He had been captured.

She gasped again, realizing the enemy had to know how important Jake was to her. No other fighter on their side had been seized and brought here. Something was about to shift the balance of power here and Ria very much feared it wouldn't be in her favor.

And then the small group with Jake stopped in front of a short man with a gray beard. Bingo. That was the source of the energy that fought to wrest control of the portal from Ria's hands. As the graybeard's attention was snagged by the group and their captive, he gave a signal and the attack slacked off.

Both the magical attack against the portal and the physical fighting within the tight confines of the stone circle slowed and then ceased altogether.

"Look, Nyx," the mage called out, facing her. "I've got your mate." He spit the word as if it was a foul thing. "Would you like to see him die?" He paused to let that sink in. "Or will you cease your resistance and save his life?"

"Don't do it," Jake grit out even as the soldiers around him forced him to his knees before the short mage.

Ria was torn. She knew her duty, but she had only just found her mate. Jake was her life. Her everything.

His head lifted and he finally met her gaze. She saw something in his eyes that gave her pause. He was up to something. She just had to have faith in him. She nodded slightly and prepared for what she had to do. What she had to say. Though it broke her heart, she had to trust in Jake and his abilities—and she had to do her duty.

It was a hell of a thing.

"What's your name, mage?" she asked, stalling for time. She positioned herself squarely in the middle of the swirling portal, just in front of it. This was, after all, her domain. The portal was the Nyx's to call and to protect.

"Master Willard Fontanbleu, as if it matters. And you're little Ria. Sold out by her uncle. Hunted all her life. Pathetic little Ria. I've searched for you for decades and now you're mine at last."

Ria laughed, though the sound was forced. There really wasn't much to laugh about at the moment, but she had to play the game. The soldiers were at a standstill, her Guard wary, but not engaged with the still forces of the mage.

"I'm my own woman to the last, Willard. As you will learn." The ancients were whispering to her, offering advice and she knew what she had to do.

"No, you little slut. You're the one who will learn. When my lady Elspeth returns she will drink your blood and use your power to summon demons and creatures from all sorts of places. Now, give up your charm and let's end this. Or I'll end him." Willard turned again to Jake, but Jake was already on the move.

And out of the dark sky, even darker shapes floated silently into the midst of the enemy forces. The dark shapes resolved into fully armed men and the scene erupted into chaos as fighting began anew.

In a blur of motion, Jake jumped to his feet. His hands were free and there was a small push dagger in one that he sank into the mage's side with a savage growl worthy of any predatory shifter.

"Now, Ria!" Jake shouted above the din of combat. He somehow knew she had the words and she spoke them as they had been given to her. Terrible words in an ancient tongue aimed at the mage who was stunned for the brief moment it took to summon his spirit to the other side.

Willard's body collapsed to its knees as the three soldiers who had subdued Jake tried to fight the whirlwind of hands, feet and knives that Jake had suddenly become. One by one, the men fell beside their leader, one dead, one dying and the other unconscious.

Meanwhile, Ria allowed the spell to work its magic, separating body from spirit and dissipating the short man's magic into the place of power in which they stood. His vast stores of magical energy drained directly into the stones and from there went into the earth. His spirit was sucked into the spinning vortex of the portal, while his body fell to the ground, an empty husk.

The battle raged as new forces entered the fray on the side of good. This had to be the mercenary group Jake had talked about. Jesse Moore's guys. The cavalry come just in the nick of time.

Ria fell to her knees beside the altar stone, a bit shocked at how easily this had all ended when the battle had been so fierce up to this point. Tears filled her eyes for the loss of life. Already many newly crossed were at the portal, speaking to her. They were speaking words of joy at the imminent victory over evil and some were talking to her, telling her not to be sad for them or feel guilt over their passing.

Eventually, after she had made note of several messages for loved ones that she promised to deliver, her mother came to speak with her. Everyone else retreated to give them a few moments alone.

"The one who was Willard was the only one who knew the Nyx's secret," her mother told her in that strong, sure voice Ria remembered from childhood. "Willard's isn't the only formerly evil soul on this side, and we have ways to deal with his issues, so don't worry. We'll take care of him now," her mother promised her. "I've already questioned him and you might be relieved to know that the rest of his order doesn't really understand what he hoped to achieve by hunting the Nyx. They think him a fool. That much is clear. So it just might be that you're a little bit safer than you have been in the past."

Ria felt a wave of relief. "Thank you," she whispered, then tried again in a stronger voice. "Thank you for helping me tonight and for being with me. Even if I haven't always taken the time to listen, I've been aware of your presence and your love. I hope you know how much you are loved in return. I miss you, mother."

"I will always miss you too, my sweetest angel," her mother said, deep emotion in her voice. "Until we meet again, which won't be for many years yet, I hope. You need time with that amazing mate of yours, and you need time to create the next generation. Ask him what he's seen about the next Nyx. I think you'll like his vision of the future."

Ria sensed the moon moving out of range. Soon the portal would close for another night. While she had one more night of this new moon tomorrow, she was never certain of who would come to speak with her. This might be the last chance she had to talk to her mother for some time. She wanted to say so much more but time was running out and she didn't know where to begin.

"Hold strong, Ria. We'll find out what we can on this side and we'll speak again tomorrow. With all that's happening in your realm and a few of the others right now, the usual strictures have been relaxed. You need help and we're finally allowed to give it in a truly meaningful way. Come back here tomorrow. Do the final ceremony of the month in the stone circle and we'll help you and the priestess cleanse this place properly. For now, go be with your mate. He needs you as much as you need him, I think."

Her mother's voice faded as the portal swished to a close, shrinking in size until it was completely gone. Only then did Ria turn around.

Jake was right behind her and her Royal Guard was directing the mop up with the help of all those who had come to help. She stepped away from the altar and into Jake's arms. They were both safe. They had made it through the battle, mostly unscathed.

She moved back to look at him, though she couldn't let him go just yet, and realized he was bleeding a bit.

"You're hurt," she noted with some anxiety. "Are you

feeling okay?"

"I'm fine, sweetheart," he smiled and pulled her back into his arms, holding her tight and rocking back and forth for a sweet, sweet moment. "I love you so much, Ria. You are the very heart of me. I've never been prouder of a person or happier at a battle won. Thank the Goddess you're safe and whole."

"I could say the same," she added, her cheek against his chest, listening to the precious beat of his heart. "I love you, Jake. I was so frightened when I saw you had been captured. How did you get your hands free?"

He moved one of her hands downward and into his back pocket. She felt a hard object which she grasped and removed from his pocket. It was a sheathed knife. A small one, in a triangular shape. The push dagger. In all probability, the same one he'd used on the mage.

"I saw my capture as one of the possibilities and I prepared for it. I usually don't carry that, but I stuck it in my back pocket earlier today just in case someone came along and tied my hands behind my back." He grinned. "Sometimes it's very helpful to know what might be coming down the road."

She smiled with him, returning the little dagger to his back pocket with a little squeeze of what had to be the finest male ass she'd ever had the good fortune to see. And it was all hers, her inner cat purred. He was her mate.

She'd yell at him later for not telling her about the possibility that he might be captured. He was going to have to learn to trust her a little more, but now…thank the Goddess…they had time.

Ria walked out of the stone circle a short while later with Jake at her side. He directed them a little south of the circle, her Guard surrounding them as they went. He had talked with the mercenary leader for quite a while, discussing what was to be done with any surviving enemy soldiers and then he'd left the cleanup of that part of the night's events in the hands of the newly-arrived soldiers and a group of the surviving fox scouts who knew the mountain ridge better than anyone.

"Just have to make a little stop," Jake claimed when he paused near a large tree that had a thicket of bushes on one side.

So much had happened in such a short amount of time. She found it hard to keep track of all the moving parts of the day. Had it been only a few hours ago that she and Jake had had one of the most intensely sexual experiences of her entire life in the middle of that stone circle? The greenery all around was stained in places now with blood and the fog of recently-ended violence filled the air.

Jake pulled a small pouch out of one of his pockets and untied the drawstring. Ria stepped closer, wanting to see what he was up to. She felt a tingle of magic in the area, but it didn't feel malevolent. If anything, it felt protective.

"What's that?" she asked as he took a pinch of what looked like small pink crystals between his thumb and forefinger. They were sort of a salmony pink and looked natural, not man-made. Each was a slightly different size and shape than the other.

"Himalayan salt, consecrated by the priestess in the snowcat stronghold. A useful thing to help friends out of a small pickle," he answered cryptically as he moved to the western side of the small circle of bushes and flicked the salt into the air.

A sparkle of magical energy showed in a dome just inside the bushes, surprising Ria and the others around them, if the little gasps of surprise were any indication.

"It's safe now," Jake said in a firm voice directed toward the dome. "You can come out. I've weakened the barrier. The rest is up to you."

Much to Ria's continued surprise, a tiger's paw struck the inside of the dome and then broke through, letting the beast land on the other side of the bushes, his tail swishing in the air. He looked back over his furry shoulder and Ria strained on her tiptoes to see over the bushes.

"Medic!" Jake shouted, stepping past the tiger with no fear, moving into the circle of bushes. He came out a moment later with an unconscious Beau Champlain in his arms.

Beau was bleeding from a very grisly-looking leg wound and Tom was in pretty bad shape from a series of cuts and gashes. Jake put Beau down while two of Ria's Guard dropped down—one on either side, already tending to his wounds. Jake went back for Tom and brought him out as well.

The tiger slunk back into the bushes and a moment later, Geir Falkes rose from inside the leafy circle, Jacki Kinkaid in his arms. She was also unconscious, but didn't look injured.

"She wore herself out casting the dome of protection," Geir said as he faced them. "Thank you for helping to break the spell. I tried to do it from within, but it was too strong."

"No problem," Jake replied modestly. "Thanks for watching over them."

"I'm taking her to the cabin. We can set up a hospital there for those who are injured. Milday," he addressed Ria directly. "Please forgive me for not being at your side. I was trapped within the dome of protection. It was wrong and I accept whatever consequences may come."

"Let's take care of the wounded first, Master Geir," Ria said wisely. "As far as I'm concerned, everything happened as it was supposed to tonight."

Geir didn't reply. He simply nodded, his lips a tight line as he turned and headed down the mountain.

He also didn't display any self-consciousness about the fact that he was nude, but then why should he? Ria watched him walk away, carrying Jacki before him, his muscular ass making a very pretty picture of male perfection as he stalked over the uneven ground.

Master Geir was as graceful on two feet as he was on four and he didn't let the rocks, sharp pine needles, and broken twigs of the forest floor slow him down. He looked like a man on a mission and nobody stood in his way as he strode silently down from the ridge in the direction of the fox stronghold.

She didn't like leaving the wounded to others' care, but she knew they were in the very best of hands. Her people would take care of them and then get them to the relative safety of the cabin as soon as possible. Meanwhile, the commandos who had parachuted in at the last minute like avenging angels were busy rounding up the last of the enemy forces and processing them.

Apparently the foxes had a cave nearby that was deep enough to house more than a few prisoners, and relatively easy to secure. Ria wanted to see the prisoners at some point. She wanted to see the kind of man who would align himself with evil. But that could wait. Tomorrow would be soon enough. For now, she wanted to go someplace safe and just be with her mate.

Escorted all the way down the ridge to the cabin, Ria was glad to see the little building hadn't been damaged in the action. She walked in, taking note of each injury and spending a few minutes with each of those who were conscious and okay to talk. She thanked them for their work there that night and delivered the messages she had been tasked to pass on from the other side.

She was glad to leave a few of the injured with lighter hearts after hearing from their loved ones. This was what the Nyx was meant to do. Offer comfort and knowledge from those who had passed on. Maybe now that the *Venifucus* had been defanged a bit, Ria could finally get back to her true calling.

She didn't know for certain that was the way it would go, but she had hope. Only a thorough interrogation of the prisoners would tell her if it was safe to think she might be out of the crosshairs for the time being. But that was for tomorrow. For the rest of tonight, now that her duties were almost completely discharged, she wanted quiet time with Jake.

The fox Alpha himself escorted her and Jake from the cabin, along with a contingent of her Royal Guard, toward the cave system. Ria stopped a few times after entering the cave system to speak with specific fox scouts who were inside, being looked after by their people—or looking after their comrades. She had a few messages for them too.

She straightened from talking to a fox woman with a gunshot graze on her shoulder and stepped under Jake's arm, settling in as they followed behind their very patient escort. The fox Alpha had left them in the capable hands of his second while he went off to coordinate care for his injured.

"Is that the last one?" Jake asked quietly as they walked deeper into the cave system.

"For now," she replied. "We'll do the final ceremony of the month tomorrow night up at the stone circle and I have a feeling they're lining up on the other side, now that they know we made it through this evening more or less intact."

"It's late. Let's find the bed the Alpha promised us and put this night behind us." For the first time that night, Jake sounded tired. Heaven knew, he had a right to be. So did she. In fact, if she thought about it at all, Ria knew she had pushed way beyond her normal reserves of strength. It was time for some restorative sleep. Past time.

The foxes had given Ria and Jake a secure chamber toward the back of the cave complex. Her Royal Guard had gone over the preparations, making sure everything was as secure as they could make it and then they withdrew. They would guard from beyond the door while she and her mate sought comfort in each other, and in the fluffy bed that seemed to be calling her name.

Ria cleaned up—sharing a quick shower with Jake that neither of them had the energy to turn into anything more than an experience in hygiene. They dried off then tumbled into the bed, wrapped in each other's arms.

And that was the last thing she knew until morning.

CHAPTER THIRTEEN

Jake woke Ria with a kiss the next morning, feeling as if the world had started spinning anew. It was like everything had been on hold until the battle and now that the conflict was resolved, things could move again.

He was truly happy for the first time in a long time. He had a woman he loved, who loved him in return and they had won a major victory in the ongoing war against evil last night. Life was good for the moment and he intended to savor it.

"Good morning," Ria murmured when he pulled back to look down into her sleepy eyes. "What time is it?"

Jake looked over at the clock on the nightstand. "Early. Probably too early to wake you up after the night we had, but I couldn't resist." He placed nibbling kisses on her collar bone as he spoke, working his way downward as he moved the blanket aside.

Ria halted his progress, pulling on his shoulders until he lifted up to gaze into her eyes. "There's somebody at the—" a loud knock sounded on the wooden door set into the stone of the cave, "—door."

"Damn," Jake groaned. "That shifter hearing of yours comes in handy," he quipped, kissing her nose with quick motions before he levered himself up to a sitting position on the side of the mattress. He looked back at her, his expression rueful as the knock sounded again. "Do we really have to answer that?"

She felt a giggle rise up in her chest. It was a joyful feeling that felt so darn good. Only recently had she felt free enough to wallow in these happy emotions. Only since meeting Jake.

"They wouldn't knock if it wasn't important," she said, knowing that duty called—or in this case, knocked.

Jake sighed and ran his fingers through his hair in an impatient, sleepy gesture. "Okay. I'll get up and see what's going on."

"You're my hero," she joked as he stood and bent, looking for his pants and giving her an excellent view of his physique while he was at it. Her inner cat wanted to purr. Then again, it always seemed to want to purr when she was with Jake. He had a potent effect on both the human and panther sides of her nature.

As it turned out, there was an urgent call from the Lords—the identical twin wolf shifters who ruled over the vast majority of werecreatures in North America. They had counterparts in many corners of the world. Most of the wolf Packs across Europe and Asia chose to be led by such beings. Identical twins were rare in the shifter world and it was thought that the Goddess chose the next rulers of each group wisely. Once in each generation, a set of identical male twins would be born and they would be raised to rule over all shifters who owed their allegiance to them.

In North America, that meant wolves, bears, cougars, foxes, various forms of raptors, and many other Tribes, Packs and Clans answered to the current twins. As such, they had a great deal of power, but because the identical twin pairs always seemed to mate with a single priestess of the Lady, they were also well-guided on their path.

Jake had never met the Lords, but Ria seemed to know them. After dressing hastily, Ria and Jake had been led into the heart of the cave complex where a communications room lay ready for their use. The fox Alpha was already there, as was the company commander of the mercenaries—a pale bear shifter who went by the name Roth—and a few others. Ria took a seat that had been left open for her directly in front of the video pickup and Jake sat at her side.

He could see the other room on the video monitors. In it were two identical men—had to be the Lords—and a pretty blonde woman who was most likely their mate. There was also a large fellow at their side who might be one of their lieutenants.

"Milady Ria," one of the twins began as soon as she was seated. "It's good to see you again. Kinkaid told us where to find you. I hope you don't mind the early call. I just remembered what time it is on the east coast. Sorry."

Ria chuckled. "It's okay. And just call me Ria," she answered with a smile and a casual wave of her hand. "This is my mate Jake." She gestured toward him.

"I'm Rafe," the first man to speak identified himself over the video connection. "You've met my brother, Tim, and our mate, Allie. This is Rocky." He nodded toward the other man on their end. "My apologies, but I didn't know you had mated. Congratulations."

"Thanks. It was a recent thing," Ria smiled and took Jake's hand on the table, making her position clear. They were a team.

"What Clan are you from, Jake?" Tim asked in a friendly yet assessing tone.

Jake shook his head. "No Clan. I'm not a shifter."

Everyone on the monitor stilled and seemed to be staring hard at the screen on their end.

"Well, what are you then? Mage?" The man named Rocky asked in a gruff voice. He didn't sound unfriendly, exactly.

Jake shook his head again. "I'm not a mage, but I am a seer. Look, we can establish my credentials very easily. Don't you know a guy named Slade? Last I heard, he was working for you. Ask him about me. He'll tell you what you need to know."

"Give us a minute." Tim reached forward and hit a button

that muted the conversation from their end.

He was then seen lifting a phone and punching in some numbers. A short conversation ensued that the folks in North Carolina couldn't hear and then Tim seemed to make a few comments to the folks on his end that made everyone's eyebrows rise a bit.

"I'd love to know what he just told them," Ria said with a grin. "Who's Slade?" she asked Jake in an almost purring tone.

He looked over at her, captivated as always, by her smile. "He's an old friend from Tibet." He almost laughed when her eyes widened, making the connection. He had just told her without words that Slade was, in all likelihood, one of the rare, mystical snowcat shapeshifters.

Tim was seen hitting the button that turned the audio back on. "Slade sends formal greetings to his brother," he said, then whistled between his teeth. "Someday I'd love to hear how you got adopted into *that* family." Clearly, Tim knew a bit about Slade's background.

"It's a long story. Maybe one day, I'll get a chance to tell it to you. For now, I'm sure my brother told you to listen for the right words, but it beats the hell out of me how I'm supposed to casually work *lotus blossom* into a sentence." Jake confirmed his identity with the code words and he saw Tim's short nod.

They got down to business after that, discussing the action of the night before and everything that had led up to it. It turned out the Lords were spearheading the North American intelligence gathering on the movements and actions of the *Venifucus* all over the country. They were also interfacing with their counterparts all over the world to build a cohesive picture of what was going on globally.

They had several high-value prisoners in detention and were using magical means to interrogate them. Roth reported what they had learned so far from the prisoners they had apprehended last night and the Lords asked if a few of the higher-ranking prisoners might be transferred to their custody. It seemed they had a high-security prison of sorts, all set up and ready to accommodate them.

Since Ria and Jake didn't have a home base and the foxes could only handle a few prisoners at a time on an ongoing basis, they agreed to the scheme. Besides, having a priestess in on the interrogations implied a lot of things. First, that the prisoners would not be mistreated. Second, that they would be given the chance to truly turn from the dark into the Light. And third, that every last harmful secret they held would eventually come out.

After the video conference drew to a close, Ria and Jake went with Roth to look over the prisoners. One thing became very clear from the reports of the interrogations so far—only the so-called Necromancer had known exactly why he was chasing the Nyx. Most of his people saw his obsession with Ria as a personal vendetta. It became obvious that Willard had boasted of powers he never really possessed as far as raising the dead or even communicating with them.

As a result, his people saw his hounding of the Nyx as his own little obsession because she could apparently do something he had tried repeatedly to do and failed. His people continued to follow him because, for all his perceived failures as a necromancer, he still had a whole lot of very specific magical power. He also held political influence in his position on the *Venifucus* Council of Elders.

Knowing they had, indeed, killed a Council member last night was a real feather in their cap. It was something nobody else could confirm having done anywhere around the world and it would most likely have dealt a severe blow to the *Venifucus* political structure. It was therefore, highly unlikely that anyone would try coming after Ria again anytime soon. If she and her people were able to take down a Council member, they were definitely a force to be reckoned with. It would take a lot of preparation and planning before anyone attempted to come after her again.

They had earned some much-needed breathing room.

There was a sense of relief and guarded happiness in the fox den all that day. Most of the foxes had made it through unscathed. They had been able to take cover in their home territory better than everyone else. Only one of the foxes had been captured, and that during the run-up to the battle.

They had retrieved that scout—a man named Zevon—and were tending to his wounds. He had been hurt badly as the enemy soldiers interrogated him, but he would live. He would need help for his wounds, both physical and psychological, but the fox Alpha had already sent out word that the non-combatants of his Pack should return to their home area. Zevon's family would look after him, smothering him with love and care, the Alpha had said. Apparently Zevon had quite a large family.

Many people were sporting bandages of one kind or another and one of the larger caverns had been set up as a hospital. Lots of gunshot wounds, but only a few were truly life-threatening. The fox Alpha had called in a go-team he had set up ahead of time that consisted of at least three doctors and several nurses and medics that were members of the fox Pack. This high up in the mountains, they had to be self-reliant and the Alpha had encouraged any of their young folk who had the desire and inclination, to go to school. As a result, this Pack had several members with advanced medical degrees earned in the human world, which came in really handy at a time like this.

In fact, the Pack owned and manned a small clinic lower down the mountain, closer to the human settlements that offered medical care for shifters and humans alike. Most of the Pack's medical personnel worked there, earning a tidy profit for the prosperous Pack and themselves.

Ria really liked what she saw of the fox Pack and the forward-thinking Alpha. He had taken his group into the twenty-first century and made it possible for them to not only survive, but thrive in the modern world.

She wondered if she might now have a chance to set up a home base and territory of her own, now that the *Venifucus* threat had been staved off. Where would she go? How would she gather the members of her Clan together? They were few and far-flung around the world. Maybe she should operate on the old movie premise—if she built it, they would come.

"You know..." she told Jake as they walked hand in hand up the mountain. It was almost time for the final new moon ceremony of the month and it was going to be done in the stone circle. "The tiger king has a stronghold built into the side of a volcano. And I heard Kinkaid has bought thousands and thousands of acres in Texas for his seat of power. Now that I'm not being hunted..." She trailed off, still hardly able to believe she might actually be free of the constant threat that had hounded her most of her life.

"Are you thinking about where to build your own nest?" Jake asked in a warm tone that made her feel loved. He was such a good man. So attuned to her moods and needs.

"*Pantera noir* isn't a Clan in the traditional sense. Not like the lions or the *tigre d'or*. In nature, there's no real equivalent to us in the animal kingdom. There is not one breed of panthers. Instead, black cats of several different species are called panthers. We're a little different. Once a big cat family breeds a *pantera noir*, they're members of our Clan. In the normal course of business, they breed true and all their progeny will be *pantera noir*. There aren't many of us, and it is seen as a mark of the Goddess's will when new *pantera noir* lines are created."

Jake nodded, seeming to contemplate her revelations. "So your Clan is small and spread out," he concluded correctly. "That kind of allows you to choose where you want to be, doesn't it? I mean, if there's no big concentration where all your people live, you can decide where to make your home more easily."

"I want to stay in the States," she said immediately. "Some of my predecessors lived at Delphi. I think they wanted a way to bring the wisdom of those who had passed to all, not just to shifters. So the Oracle at Delphi was a good place for them, then. The world is a lot different now and the rules around what those on the other side can tell me have changed along the way." She thought about her mother's words from last night and paused slightly. "Although…I think they may have just changed again after last night. My mother said as much when she told me to do the ceremony up in the stone circle again tonight."

They walked along in silence for a moment, making progress up the wooded trail. Her Guards were with them, of course, but keeping a perimeter that allowed Ria and Jake a sense of privacy. Her people were amazing. Many had been injured in various ways in the battle, but all those who were mobile were already back at their posts—even though she'd told them to take it easy. She'd finally had to ask Master Geir to evaluate everyone personally and order those who needed more healing time to take it.

"Do you have any particular State in mind for your home base?" Jake asked, restarting the conversation a few moments later.

"Not really. Do you?" She looked up at him in the twilight. The moon would rise earlier tonight and she wanted to be in the circle well ahead of time to be sure all was ready.

"Well, my sister went back upstate New York when she married Cade. Since Gina's folks moved back to Iceland, they might be willing to sell us their place. It's a fortress, from what I hear, and built to suit cats who like to roam. Plus, Cade and Ellie are already in the area. Maybe more of your Clan could be enticed to join us, considering the tigers did all the heavy lifting creating the place."

"That's a brilliant idea!" She felt joy leap in her heart when she thought about his suggestion. It made a lot of sense and the stronghold she'd thought about building over many years was already there. "We'd make our own changes, of course, but the framework is already in place and the area is already clear for shifters. Plus, I think most of the tigers really just wanted to go back to Iceland. Ellie said a lot of the area was empty now. Could be a lot of tigers willing to sell out to us. Oh, I like this."

Ria leaned in to hug Jake around the waist as they walked along. He really was perfect for her in every way. Thanks be to the Goddess that they'd made it through the battle last night and had hope for a better future.

Ria conducted the new moon ceremony a short while later, surrounded by most of those who were mobile enough to join them. Many messages were delivered to individuals who responded in varying ways—some with tears, some with joy, some with solemn dignity. When the public portion of the evening was over and those who had come to receive messages had taken them and left, Ria had a chance to talk with her mother once more.

"You are safe for now, sweetheart," her mother confirmed. "But the entire world isn't safe yet from the Destroyer. The *Venifucus* will continue to look for ways to free Elspeth and return her to the mortal realm. You're going to have to be vigilant. Your mate's idea about buying the tiger's former stronghold in the mountains of New York is a really good one. It will be a good place for the Clan to gather. Strength in numbers, Ria. It's not a good time to be a loner."

Her mother imparted a few more words of wisdom before the moon moved on and their time ran out for this month. Ria hoped that by next month, she would be doing the ceremony in her own home. Although…anywhere Jake was, was home. Still, she'd always wanted a stronghold…

They walked back to the fox den and stayed the night. Jake spent an hour or two talking strategy with Ben, Geir, Seth, and Roth, leader of the company of Moore's soldiers who had stuck around for the mop up. They were planning to evac some of the higher-value prisoners to the Lords' mountain in Montana and other places where they could be housed and interrogated more completely over time. The conditions were humane, but nobody was sure yet if these men could be released. They would have to be carefully examined by priestesses and other folk who would be able to tell if the men were simple soldiers or something even more dangerous.

While Jake was closeted with the military component, Ria spent her time visiting the injured and talking with her friends among her Royal Guard. It was good to be at ease, for once, with no danger breathing down their necks. The mood among her people had lightened, even though many were injured and several would take a long time to heal.

That the number of deaths on their side was so low was a minor miracle. Then again, they'd had time to prepare and the fox scouts had shared their knowledge of the terrain freely with her people. Though she hadn't spent much time among their kind before, she had gained new respect for the breed and saw the truth of the old adage about being *clever like a fox*. Some of the hidey holes they'd revealed around the mountain were downright ingenious, and had come in very handy in keeping casualties to a minimum.

Ria headed back to the room they'd been given, deep inside the fox den with only a pair of her Royal Guard keeping her company. She liked having them around, but now that she was mated to Jake, she craved more privacy to share with her lover. Life had changed in a big way and she was still trying to figure out what it would all mean to the way they moved forward.

Would she be able to settle down now? Would they have a home of their own? In one place. Not having to flee all the time and stay on the move. It was quite a concept to a woman who had lived most of her life on the run. She craved the stability of a home of her own.

Now that she was mated, she craved a den. A nest she could feather and prepare for the next generation. She wanted a family. Maybe not right away, but eventually. She wanted to raise her cubs in security and teach the daughter she hoped to have about the responsibility of their lineage.

It was a nice dream. A simple dream. And one she was finally able to believe in. Since Jake had swept into her life, so much had changed. That they might actually have a shot at the fabled *happily ever after* was still something that was a bit like a fantasy to her. A fantasy she wanted to reach out and grab with both hands. And never let go.

It all began and ended with her mate. Jake.

With a smile on her lips, Ria decided to surprise him as she entered their bedroom. Her Guards would remain in the hallway, doing their duty, but inside this room—and the connecting bath…and the little surprise the fox Alpha had finally told her about a couple of hours ago—they were alone. Man and woman. Mates. Forever.

It was time to start their honeymoon. Finally.

Ria shed her clothing and shifted her shape into the other half of her being. The cat who lived within. Feeling rather decadent and daring, she stretched out on the big bed, and waited for her mate to come to her.

Jake scratched his nose as he opened the door to their bedroom. He stopped short, seeing the giant black cat stretched out across the bed, his hand stilling and then dropping to his side. After a beat, he continued into the room and closed the door behind himself, leaving the two Royal Guards on duty on either side of the portal. He'd have to get used to having them around. Just as he'd have to get used to coming back and finding his mate in her fur coat.

Man, she was something. Lethal and slinky. Gorgeous and sexy. Powerful and…his. Just his. When that thought hit, Jake realized all over again how much of a lucky bastard he really was.

He approached the bed, noting the languid golden gaze that followed his every movement. He sat on the side of the bed, lowering one hand to stroke the flank of the silky creature that was his mate. He could feel the rumble and hear the sound as she began to purr and he had to smile.

"You are the most gorgeous creature I have ever seen—in your fur and out of it, Ria."

In a shimmer of darkness, the cat disappeared to be replaced by a beautiful, very naked woman. Ria. His mate. From stroking the cat's fur, his fingers went to the softness of her pale skin, his hand pausing at the curve of her hip.

"One of us has too many clothes on and I don't think it's me," she said teasingly as she gazed up at him.

"You know, I think you're right. But not to worry." He stood up and reached started tugging at his T-shirt, pulling it off over his head and tossing it across the room. "That problem can be remedied shortly."

Ria stood and reached for his belt, drawing closer to his body in a way that pushed every one of his buttons. Damn, the woman knew what he liked already and they hadn't even been together that long. Jake could only imagine how good they would be together in the years to come. He was almost eager to realize that vision, but he didn't want to miss out on any of the learning it took to get from here to there. He vowed to enjoy the ride, this mating to a shifter queen.

She tugged his belt loose, then started right in on his fly as her lips drifted closer, playing over his collar bones and upper chest. When she licked him, he almost jumped. His cock definitely did, twitching within the confines of the denim she was quickly removing.

When she freed him, she didn't push his pants down all the way right away. Instead, she paused a moment to take him in her hands, squeezing as she held his gaze. Her golden eyes teased him, her touch tantalized and he grew hard within her hands as she rubbed him just the right way.

But then she let go and turned away. Jake started after her, but had to stop because his pants were hampering his movements. It would look ridiculous if he fell on his ass right in front of her. So he stopped and slid the jeans off, pausing only for a moment to rid himself of his shoes and socks as well. He looked up to find her watching him over her shoulder, her long hair sliding sexily down her back. Damn, she was beautiful.

"Now we're evenly matched," he said, hoping to lure her back. He wasn't sure where she was going, but he was eager to follow.

"It's a start," she agreed, flouncing her hair as she turned her head and kept walking. He realized then that she had been moving toward the large bathroom that was attached to their suite.

It was a beautiful room, done in earth tones like the rest of the cave complex, but with all the modern conveniences. There was hot and cold running water and lighting. Electric outlets for hair dryers and all that kind of thing. Everything a modern shifter could want—all underground.

And there was no missing the fact that they were underground. The walls were round. Like a little dome had been dug out of the mountain over time.

Ria stepped into the bathtub, which had been carved out of the rock of the mountain, but there wasn't any water in it. Jake wondered what she was up to when she reached out to touch not the handles that would bring forth water, but the spigot from which it should run. She lifted the spigot in a way a spigot should not be able to move and the back wall of the tub slid away to reveal another chamber beyond.

"What the heck...?" Jake wondered even as Ria smiled and stepped over the rim and into the small cavern she had just revealed.

"The Alpha told me about this earlier today. Said it was a little gift from him to us for our new mating. This is his private hideaway," she explained. "I didn't realize it before, but he gave us his own room to sleep in. His mate is still with the women and children who were evacuated, so he's been bunking down in a guest room so we'd have the best place in the den. Isn't that sweet of him?"

"RHIP," Jake muttered. She looked at him funny so he interpreted. "Rank Has Its Privileges. Something I learned in the Marine Corps."

Ria laughed and moved farther into the secret room. "He said there's a hot spring in here as well as a little trickle of fresh, cold water. All the comforts of home and a convenient place to hide should the den be overrun somehow." She looked around as she walked into the cavern. It was much more cave-looking than the rest of the suite had been. Closer to nature. More primal.

She moved deeper into the room. Her Guard wouldn't be happy that she had entered a room they hadn't checked first, but what they didn't know...

"Ah. There is it." She turned into a little hollow and sure enough, there was a bit of mist hanging over a small pool of clear water.

It bubbled toward the far end and she could see the steam rising into a small fissure that led upward through the mountain. It was well ventilated, which kept the ambient moisture at a minimum. Ria dipped a toe in and found the temperature to be warm, but not too hot. In fact, it was just about perfect.

"This is man-made," Jake observed, noting the square shape of the pool by making a square in the air with his fingers.

"The Alpha pair's secret getaway," she confirmed. "He built it for his mate as a gift. There was always a hot spring here, but it was smaller. He hollowed out the pool himself over time, expanding it to what you see here now."

"It drains and recirculates," Jake added, seeming more interested in the plumbing for the moment than he was in her. Ria would have to change that.

She slid into the hot, clear water, dunking her head and then coming up to let the water stream down her back, pulling her hair back from her face. She stood in the shallow pool, the water only about thigh-deep. She felt the hot water dripping off her pointed breasts, rolling down her skin. She opened her eyes and was gratified to see she had Jake's full and complete attention once again.

"Care to join me?" She felt the purr in her words, hoping it was something he liked. She couldn't really control her animal responses to her mate. She only hoped she didn't scare him away.

"I'd love to," he growled. She realized then that he wasn't turned off. Far from it.

He stepped down into the pool, moving straight for her. She didn't move away. She let him take her into his arms and met his mouth in a fiery kiss that stole her breath. His cock rode hard against her belly and she knew the first time wasn't going to be a long, drawn out affair. No, this would be primal—just like this place. There would be time for a more delicate joining later. This one had to be hard and fast.

Ria moved backward as Jake followed, his body rubbing against her at every step, his lips on hers, his mouth doing things to hers that made her pulse beat a hard tattoo against her skin. She found the ledge with the backs of her legs and pulled on Jake's shoulders to coax him to follow her downward. He followed her lead and soon they were sitting in about a foot and a half of water on a part of the pool that sloped upward so that even if Ria leaned all the way back, her head would be above water, while the rest of her body was below it.

The position had possibilities. She had never made love underwater before and it seemed like now was the perfect time to try it out. Then again, she wanted to try anything and everything with her new mate, but for now, this would do.

"Take me now, Jake. I don't want to wait," she urged him the moment he released her lips.

He pulled back slightly to look deep into her eyes. "Are you sure?"

She nodded eagerly. "Fast the first time. We can go slower the second. Or maybe the third." Her smile teased and he responded in kind.

"How about the fourth?" He moved over her in the warm water, taking his place between her thighs as she spread for him.

"Oh? Confident are we?" She laughed and then gasped as he slid into her body, the warm water creating new and exciting sensations all over her skin and easing his path even more than usual.

"You make me feel like a superhero, Ria." His voice dipped low as he nibbled on her neck, just below her ear and began to move in a slow, easy rhythm.

"You are, Jake. You're my superhero," she replied solemnly, biting her lip as the pleasure increased with his pace.

"Okay," he drew back, stilling and looking down into her eyes. "But I refuse to wear a cape."

She burst out laughing and he groaned as her inner muscles clenched on him.

"Oh, baby, you're killing me," he groused as he began moving again, faster than before, causing little wavelets to erupt on the surface of the water around her. It made the water lap against her sensitive breasts, caressing her in warm wetness that was incredibly comforting...and stimulating.

She shrieked as a little climax broke over her and then built right away again into something more. Jake kept moving, kept increasing his pace as little orgasms hit her one after another. Her body had never done that before, but it was delicious. She wanted more and Jake didn't disappoint.

He pushed into her, using the buoyancy of the water to aid his cause, easing his grip and letting her body float a bit while he thrust deep in and out again, the warmth of the water creating sensations against her skin that she had never felt before in passion. It was like being wrapped in velvet and stroked all over, and inside out. Ria's cries grew louder as she came and came, each little wave breaking over her senses higher than the last.

Finally, after too many climaxes to count, Jake pushed her over the edge one final time, into oblivion. She heard him shout her name as he followed her into bliss, but that was all she knew for a few minutes. His loving had caused her to pass out.

Ria woke with a smile on her face a few moments later. Jake was still with her, his weight nothing to complain about with the water supporting them both. She loved the closeness of their bond, the freedom she felt with him that she had never felt before. He was her everything now, and she looked forward to her future for the first time in a long time because she would be sharing it with him. And with their cubs, in the fullness of time.

"You okay?" he asked in a gravelly voice near her ear.

"Never better," she replied with a loving, satisfied smile.

"You're my world, Ria," he whispered, giving her a little squeeze with his strong arms.

"I love you, Jake. Forever."

"I love you too, Ria. Forever."

They made love in and out of the water throughout the rest of the night, sleeping in short stretches only to wake and make love again. It was the first night of their honeymoon after all, and it seemed a shame to waste the ambiance and amenities of the Alpha's secret hideaway.

Early the next morning, Ria and Jake were in the communications room in the fox den, placing a secure call to Iceland. They said hello to Mitch, then got down to haggling with Mitch's new father-in-law.

It wasn't much of a haggle, though. The older tiger was very happy to come to terms with Ria and Jake over the home he no longer needed in New York. He and his wife had moved back to Iceland after a long exile and didn't want to go back to the States to live. They did reserve the right of safe-passage and shelter, should it ever become necessary. They also brought Mitch into the discussions to formalize and renew the alliance between their Clans.

It was a good deal all around. Ria and Jake had a safe place to live and the tigers didn't have to worry about their old place laying empty. Arrangements were made for a team of tigers to meet Ria and Jake at the compound and show them all the hidden secrets of the land and the buildings.

As it turned out, many of the outbuildings and houses lower down on the mountain that the former tiger king-in-exile had owned, were also up for sale by members of his Clan. They were compiling a list of places and individuals to contact. Ria would put out the word through the Clan grapevine that she was going to settle in New York and that any who wanted should gather with her. Mitch appointed one of his offices in New York—the tiger Clan had a lot of business interests all over the world—to facilitate the real estate transactions.

They had an understanding in less than an hour and paperwork would commence immediately. Before they'd ended the call, Master Geir—who had been standing in the room, doing his duty as a Guard—interrupted to say that he already knew which property he was interested in.

As Master of the Nyx's Royal Guard he had been in touch with others in his position. He said he knew the Millers, who had trained the *tigre d'or* Royal Guard. Apparently the Miller family owned a big spread that included a state of the art dojo which could easily accommodate the entire Guard corps and anyone else who might seek training with him.

Mitch knew Geir, of course, from his days as a Royal Guard, and was only too happy to speak to the Millers on his behalf. So it looked like not only did Ria and Jake have a stronghold, but a garrison set to defend it. All in the space of a few short hours. All they needed to do was go there and take possession, set things up to their liking, and...live.

Ria looked forward to it with every fiber of her being. To be at peace, for even a short while. To just live in one place and not worry about being hunted... It was like a miracle.

Oh, they still had enemies. She knew that well enough. And there might still be battles with the *Venifucus* on the horizon, but for at least the foreseeable future, they could make a home. A permanent home. It was a novelty.

"If I asked you what you foresaw for our future in New York, what would you say?" she asked Jake playfully when they were alone, packing their few belongings from the room they had used in the fox den.

Jake looked up at her, then came over and pulled her into his arms. "That's easy. All I see when I look into our future, my dearest love, is happiness."

# # #

ABOUT THE AUTHOR

Bianca D'Arc has run a laboratory, climbed the corporate ladder in the shark-infested streets of lower Manhattan, studied and taught martial arts, and earned the right to put a whole bunch of letters after her name, but she's always enjoyed writing more than any of her other pursuits. She grew up and still lives on Long Island, where she keeps busy with an extensive garden, several aquariums full of very demanding fish, and writing her favorite genres of paranormal, fantasy and sci-fi romance.

Bianca loves to hear from readers and can be reached through Twitter (@BiancaDArc), Facebook (BiancaDArcAuthor) or through the various links on her website.

WELCOME TO THE D'ARC SIDE…
WWW.BIANCADARC.COM

OTHER BOOKS BY BIANCA D'ARC

Now Available

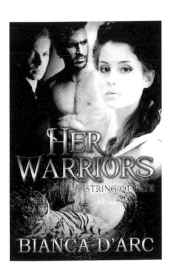

STRING OF FATE
HER WARRIORS

Love triangles are always more interesting when they come equipped with claws…and flippers?

Beau has anger issues, but not when he's around Jacki. The fierce tiger shifter has been following her around like a puppy, but she hasn't taken notice of him…until now.

No matter how long Geir has lived in the States, he's still the odd man out. A tiger shifter native of Iceland, he is a Master of his craft, training other warriors the skills he has perfected. When he sees Jacki for the first time, he knows she is the one for him.

Jacki is the daughter of a prominent shifter Clan. Most of her relatives are lion shifters, so she knows how to handle cats on the prowl, but she is a selkie—a seal shifter—imbued with magic and surrounded by mystery. When she's told she doesn't have to choose between the two tigers, but can have them both, she is intrigued.

But someone is stalking their path and they must work together to nullify the danger, all while trying to figure out a complicated relationship that has all three of them questioning fate.

Warning: This story contains graphic language and menage a trois between two tiger shifters and one very special selkie woman. Rawr.

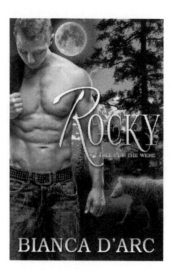

TALES OF THE WERE ~ THE OTHERS
ROCKY

On the run from her husband's killers, there is only one man who can help her now… her Rock.

Maggie is on the run from those who killed her husband nine months ago. She knows the only one who can help her is Rocco, a grizzly shifter she knew in her youth. She arrives on his doorstep in labor with twins. Magical, shapeshifting, bear cub twins destined to lead the next generation of werecreatures in North America.

Rocky is devastated by the news of his Clan brother's death, but he cannot deny the attraction that has never waned for the small human woman who stole his heart a long time ago. Rocky absented himself from her life when she chose to marry his childhood friend, but the years haven't changed the way he feels for her.

And now there are two young lives to protect. Rocky will do everything in his power to end the threat to the small family and claim them for himself. He knows he is the perfect Alpha to teach the cubs as they grow into their power… if their mother will let him love her as he has always longed to do.

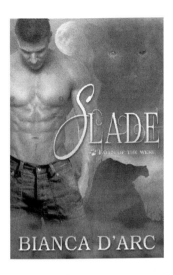

TALES OF THE WERE ~ THE OTHERS
SLADE

The fate of all shifters rests on his broad shoulders, but all he can think of is her.

Slade is a warrior and spy sent to Nevada to track a brutal murderer before the existence of all shifters is revealed to a world not ready to know.

Kate is a priestess serving the large community of shifters that have gathered around the Redstone cougars. When their matriarch is murdered and the scene polluted by dark magic, she knows she must help the enigmatic man sent to track the killer.

Together, Slade and Kate find not one but two evil mages that they alone can neutralize. Slade finds it hard to keep his hands off his sexy new partner, the cougars are out for blood, and the killers have an even more sinister plan in mind.

Can Kate somehow keep her hands to herself when the most attractive man she's ever met makes her want to throw caution to the wind? And can Slade do his job and save the situation when he's finally found a woman who can make him purr?

Warning: Contains a tiny bit of sexy ménage action with two smokin' hot men..

TALES OF THE WERE ~ REDSTONE CLAN 1
GRIF

Griffon Redstone is the eldest of five brothers and the leader of one of the most influential shifter Clans in North America. He seeks solace in the mountains, away from the horrific events of the past months, for both himself and his young sister. The deaths of their older sister and mother have hit them both very hard.

Lindsey Tate is human, but very aware of the werewolf Pack that lives near her grandfather's old cabin. She's come to right a wrong her grandfather committed against the Pack and salvage what's left of her family's honor—if the wolves will let her. Mostly, they seem intent on running her out of town on a rail.

But the golden haired stranger, Grif, comes to her rescue more than once. He stands up for her against the wolf Pack and then helps her fix the old generator at the cabin. When she performs a ceremony she expects will end in her death, the shifter deity has other ideas. Thrown together by fate, neither of them can deny their deep attraction, but will an old enemy tear them apart?

Warning: Frisky cats get up to all sorts of naughtiness, including a frenzy-induced multi-partner situation that might be a little intense for some readers.

TALES OF THE WERE ~ REDSTONE CLAN 2
RED

A water nymph and a werecougar meet in a bar fight… No joke.

Steve Redstone agrees to keep an eye on his friend's little sister while she's partying in Las Vegas. He's happy to do the favor for an old Army buddy. What he doesn't expect is the wild woman who heats his blood and attracts too much attention from Others in the area.

Steve ends up defending her honor, breaking his cover and seducing the woman all within hours of meeting her, but he's helpless to resist her. She is his mate and that startling fact is going to open up a whole can of worms with her, her brother and the rest of the Redstone Clan.

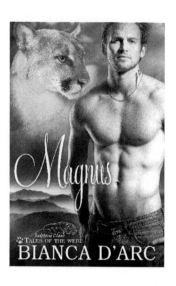

TALES OF THE WERE ~ REDSTONE CLAN 3
MAGNUS

A tortured vampire, a lonely shifter, and a deadly power struggle of supernatural proportions. Can their forbidden love prevail?

Magnus is the quiet brother. The one who keeps to himself. But he has good reason for his loner status. Two years ago, he met a woman. Not just any woman. This woman made his inner cougar stand up and roar. Even in human form, he purred when she stroked him, a sure sign that she was his mate. And mating is a very serious thing among shifters. Too bad the lady had fangs...

Mag discovers Miranda being held captive. She's been tortured to the point of -madness. Mag frees her and takes her to his home, nursing her back to health and defying all convention to keep her with him. He doesn't ever want to let her go again, but he knows the deck is stacked against them.

When a vampire uprising threatens, Mag and Miranda are in the middle. More than just their necks are on the line when a group of vampires seek to kill them and overthrow the current Master. But they have powerful allies, and their renewed relationship has made both of them stronger than either would ever be alone.

Can they stay together forever? Or will the daylight—and their two very different worlds—tear them apart again?

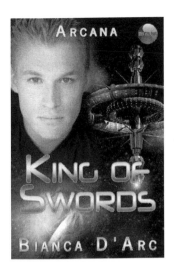

ARCANA
KING OF SWORDS

David is a newly retired special ops soldier, looking to find his way in an unfamiliar civilian world. His first step is to visit an old friend, the owner of a bar called *The Rabbit Hole* on a distant space station. While there, he meets an intriguing woman who holds the keys to his future.

Adele has a special ability, handed down through her family. Adele can sometimes see the future. She doesn't know exactly why she's been drawn to the space station where her aunt deals cards in a bar that caters to station workers and ex-military. She only knows that she needs to be there. When she meets David, sparks of desire fly between them and she begins to suspect that he is part of the reason she traveled halfway across the galaxy.

Pirates gas the inhabitants of the station while Adele and David are safe inside a transport tube and it's up to them to repel the invaders. Passion flares while they wait for the right moment to overcome the alien threat and retake the station. But what good can one retired soldier and a civilian do against a ship full of alien pirates?

WWW.BIANCADARC.COM

10222212R00112

Printed in Great Britain
by Amazon.co.uk, Ltd.,
Marston Gate.